The Firehills

The Firehills

STEVE ALTON

 Carolrhoda Books, Inc. • Minneapolis

I would like to thank my wife, Karin, as ever; Dr. David Morfitt, for excellent advice on all things historical; Jack Todhunter, who continues to teach me; my team of volunteer readers—Sharon, Flo, and Anne; and the people of the town of Hastings, for keeping the spirit of Jack-in-the-Green alive.

Carolrhoda Books, Inc.
A division of Lerner Publishing Group
241 First Avenue North
Minneapolis, MN 55401 U.S.A.

Website address: www.lernerbooks.com

Library of Congress Cataloging-in-Publication Data

Alton, Steve.
     The Firehills / by Steve Alton.
        p.   cm.
     Summary: Charly, a recently initiated Wiccan, and her friend Sam reunite at the Green Man Festival in England, and this time find themselves battling the Sidhe, ancient faeries who are trying to conquer the world.
     ISBN-13: 978-1-57505-798-9 (lib. bdg. : alk. paper)
     ISBN-10: 1-57505-798-0 (lib. bdg. : alk. paper)
     [1. Magic—Fiction. 2. Wizards—Fiction. 3. Witches—Fiction. 4. Fairies—Fiction. 5. Space and time—Fiction. 6. England—Fiction.] I. Title.
PZ7.A466Fir 2005
[Fic]—dc22   2005007507

Manufactured in the Unites States of America
1 2 3 4 5 6 – BP – 11 10 09 08 07 06

For Ben

author's note

Legends of a nonhuman race, inhabiting the land since ancient times and possessing magical powers, are common among the Celtic peoples of northern Europe. They were variously known as elves, fairies (or faeries), the Good People, or the Gentry. In Gaelic they were called the Sidhe—pronounced SHEE—which was also the word for wind. For this reason, they were known as the People of the Wind. The Sidhe may be the same race as the Tuatha de Danaan—pronounced THOO-a-hah day DAH-nawn. These people traditionally lived in Ireland before the invasion of the Milesians, a Gaelic tribe from Spain.

She is of the Tuatha de Danaan who are unfading . . . and I am of the Sons of Mil, who are perishable and fade away.

—Caeilte of the Fianna,
in *The Colloquy of the Ancients*

prologue

Sam stood on the worn grass of the playing field, his coat collar turned up and his hands thrust deep in his pockets. High above him, a lone kestrel hung in the wind, a dark speck against the hard blue sky.

Sam shifted the focus of his mind, and suddenly he was looking down on himself, a hunched figure far below, dark against the green grass. Gazing out through the kestrel's wild yellow eyes, he felt the play of wind along the surfaces of its wings. Its tail feathers flexed and shifted as it battled to hold its position in the face of the gale. Easing himself into the hot flicker of the bird's mind, Sam *became* the kestrel, giving himself over to its fierce instincts as he scanned the grass for signs of prey. The gusting wind sent ripples through the chestnut feathers of his back. In an ecstasy of sky and air, he opened his beak and gave a high, harsh cry.

Hanging there against the blue, he thought about how his life had changed since the events of the previous summer. Before that vacation—and his fateful encounter with the bard Amergin—life had been so simple. His greatest challenge had been to finish the latest computer game, his most serious concern how to avoid his parents and their endless museum visits. And then he had awakened Amergin from an ancient sleep and found himself plunged into a world he had never imagined. A world where dark creatures stalked the land, and magic filled the air. Hailed as a long-awaited hero, he stumbled from crisis to crisis, aided by Amergin and Charly, his newfound friends. In the end, though, he had been alone. His strange encounter with the Green Man and the final, desperate battle with the ancient evil of the Malifex had taken place far from any aid.

And so it should have ended. Wasn't that how it happened in books, after all? The bad guy destroyed, the world saved, the hero returned from the field of battle? Everything is back to normal. Except . . . something remained. The Green Man was gone, as was his evil twin, the Malifex. Their power was dispersed, back into the land from which they had been born. But something lingered from Sam's encounter. When he had taken on the Green Man's powers for that short time, some bond had been formed. If that power was dispersed, then some of it, at least, lingered around Sam and marked him out as *different*. An outsider—a stranger in his own world.

Off in the far distance, a bell rang, and instantly Sam was back in his own body once more. The kestrel, free of his control, wheeled out over the chain-link fence that marked the boundary of the playing field and was soon lost to view.

With a sigh, Sam turned and began the walk back to the line of school buildings, gray and unwelcoming in the distance.

chapter 1

Megan bustled around her workshop, humming under her breath. An assortment of cardboard boxes stood on the workbenches, shredded paper spilling out of them and on to the floor. She paused before a shelf, glasses perched on the end of her nose, and peered at the line of pottery faces. Tucking a strand of auburn hair behind her ear, she selected three and carried them over to a box, where she nestled them gently among the paper strands. The door clicked open, and Charly burst in, jumping down the steps and giving her mother a brief hug.

"How's it going?" Charly asked.

"Getting there," replied Megan. "Just a few more of the Green Man plates, then I'm all packed."

"Shame." Charly grinned. "I was going to offer to help. Amergin's leaping round the living room helping Buffy slay vampires. I thought it might be safer out here."

"A holiday will do him good. He's going square-eyed in front of that TV. Are you looking forward to our little trip?" Megan asked knowingly.

"Yeah, I suppose," replied Charly casually.

"Looking forward to seeing Sam again?"

"Mu-um!" Charly blushed. "I'm going. I'll take my chances with Amergin. Give me a shout, and I'll help you load the car."

"Even better," replied Megan, "send Square-eyes out here to give me a hand."

A few minutes later, the workshop door clicked open once more, and Megan glanced round, smiling. A tall, middle-aged man was framed in the doorway, piercing eyes beneath a sweep of graying hair. Closing the door behind him, he dropped lightly down the short flight of steps and strode across the room.

Megan detected an air of excitement about Amergin as he bent and kissed the top of her head. "Go on," she said with a sigh, "What now?"

Amergin's face broke into a grin. "I have seen a man of the most amazing powers! Superhuman strength, astonishing speed, the ability to see through solid matter! And all this used in the service of justice—"

"Did he have a red and blue costume?" asked Megan wearily.

"Yes!" exclaimed the wizard. "That's the very man!"

"Superman. That would be Superman."

"Fiction?" asked Amergin, looking crestfallen.

Megan nodded.

"I thought as much." Amergin sighed. "Oh, well. I must return," he continued, brightening. "Buffy's on!"

Ever since Amergin had awakened from his ancient sleep in the burial mound on Brenscombe Hill behind Megan's farm in Dorset, he had been like a child in a sweetshop. Everything around him was fresh and new, and his keen mind soaked up information from every available source. Television was his great passion. Megan was becoming concerned that he was receiving too much information too soon. The wizard lacked the background knowledge to separate fact from fiction, great drama from soap opera.

Megan watched his retreating back as he clattered up the steps, already practicing his vampire-slaying moves. She smiled to herself, tucked the strand of hair behind her ear once more, and returned to her packing.

 ✝

In ones and twos, they made their way along the narrow streets of the town. Without seeming to try, they kept to the shadows. Only rarely did the orange glare of a streetlight fall on pale skin or glint on silver jewelry. The late-night holiday visitors making the circuit of pubs and clubs barely noticed them. Such sights were common. Every town had Goths, groups of surly youths and sullen teenagers, rebelling against conformity by dressing alike— black hair, black clothes, black looks in pale skin.

From across the town they came, converging on a small door in an otherwise featureless expanse of brick wall. A dull, rhythmic thudding seemed to come from beneath the flagstones of the pavement. Above the door, a spidery sign in purple neon flickered on and off: The Crypt.

Down a winding flight of stairs, past blank-faced security staff they paced, bolder now that they were underground. With a contemptuous push, the final doors swung open, and they plunged gratefully into their element.

The noise here was deafening, a relentless pulsing felt in the chest as much as heard, making conversation almost impossible. Smoke and dry ice hung in the air, lit by the staccato flicker of a strobe light. Black-clad figures stood in small groups or huddled around tables, staring into the smoke or down at the stained purple carpet. One or two looked up as the double doors swung open once more and the latest arrivals made their entrance.

A man and a young woman strode across the room, and many pairs of eyes followed them. The furtive air that had marked them in the streets above was gone now. They walked with their heads high, he with a look of fierce ownership, she with an amused half-smile. He wore black leather pants and a baggy white shirt, collarless and unbuttoned to mid-chest. Its flaring cuffs emerged from the sleeves of a long, flowing black overcoat. She wore what seemed to be a wedding dress, a sweeping creation of silk and lace complete with veil and train but all of it as black as midnight. Collecting drinks from the bar, Finnvarr and Lady Una moved to join a group leaning against a mirror-tiled pillar and took up their positions. After exchanging nods with their companions, they stood in apparent silence, faces expressionless once more, seemingly lost in the pounding music. But between their minds, a mental conversation flickered like summer lightning.

Welcome, my lord, thought one of the figures against the pillar, staring with apparent boredom at the dance floor.

Welcome. Aye, welcome, chorused the others.

Finnvarr inclined his head slightly in acknowledgment. His consort favored the group with a smirk.

What news, my lord? inquired a girl with black lips and a mane of purple hair.

We failed once more, came the mental response, cold and clear. *Some power blocks us—I feel it. It is strong, but somehow . . . I cannot see it. It is hidden from me.*

But how can that be? asked a thin youth with a narrow face and a sneering mouth. *No sorcerer remains who could resist us!*

Fool! snapped the Lord of the Sidhe, the look of boredom dropping from his face for a moment. The sneering youth quailed, his eyes downcast. *Do you dare to tell me my business?* Regaining his composure, he continued. *Some great power of the Elder Days lingers on. I feel it hovering on the edge of my reach. Something or someone acts as a focus for that power and blocks our efforts. We will never take up the mantle of the Dark One while ever that power remains.*

A mortal, my lord? asked another.

The Lord of the Sidhe shook his head, the mane of black and purple hair twitching around his shoulders. *Mortals lack the discipline. Who among them would oppose us? These weekend witches with their crystals and trinkets? Real estate agents and housewives, with their suburban covens? No, none remain who truly comprehend the Old Ways. Their kind is gone.*

Then who?

I do not know. But I will find out. Send out word to our brethren: Continue the search. Leave no stone unturned. Whoever—or whatever—stands in our way will be found. And then I will crush them. This land will fall beneath the dominion of the Sidhe.

The mental conversation died away, leaving no trace on the blank faces. Only the girl in the black wedding dress allowed herself a smile, as the strobe lights flickered and stabbed through the smoke.

⊹

Charly skipped through the small herb garden that separated the workshop from the bulk of the cottage. Though she would never admit it to her mother, she was excited about their trip, and it was largely the prospect of seeing Sam again. Every year, Megan went to Hastings on the southeast coast to sell her pottery at the Jack-in-the-Green Festival, held in the ruined castle. This year, knowing that Sam and his parents lived close by, Megan had suggested that perhaps Sam might like to join them in Hastings for a few days. After all, Jack-in-the-Green was another name for the Green Man. Sam should be keen to see the festival for himself.

Charly had groaned and squirmed, but inside she was hoping and praying that Sam's parents would agree. When a letter had arrived thanking Megan for her kind offer, Charly had taken herself off to her favorite spot—a cluster of prehistoric burial mounds on the hill behind the farm—and in the thin spring sunshine danced her thanks to the Goddess.

The weeks had passed in painful slow motion, but gradually the days lengthened, and April blossomed into May. And now the weekend was finally here. Charly let herself into the house, avoided the lunging figure of Amergin as he battled the undead from his perch on the sofa, and headed for her room to pack.

They set off very early the next morning. It was a long journey, and Megan would have to do all the driving. Amergin had expressed a desire to learn, but both Megan and Charly thought it would be wise to wait. The wizard was still too fascinated by everything he saw around him to be capable of keeping his eyes on the road. Amergin sat in the front passenger seat, and as they made their way eastward, he traced their progress on a series of large and unwieldy maps, chattering excitedly.

Just before midday, Megan spotted something that made her brake suddenly and swerve off the road into a field entrance. Off to the south was a gently sloping hillside of spring barley—fresh green and waving in the wind. Megan jumped out of the car and stood on the shoulder of the road, gazing out across the field. Charly and Amergin clambered out to join her.

"A crop circle!" exclaimed Charly.

"Mmm," said her mother, "odd."

"It's wicked!" replied Charly. She loved crop circles, and this was a particularly fine example, a huge central circle of flattened stems, throwing off spiral arms of smaller circles, decreasing in size as they swirled away into the field.

"Yes. Yes, it's nice," agreed Megan, "but it's the wrong time of year."

"How do you mean?"

"It just seems a bit early. Crop circles usually appear closer to harvesttime, when the crop's nearly ripe, though

19

I've heard of circles in canola as early as May before. I don't know. They seem to be getting more and more frequent these days. It's probably all the hoaxers."

"Ladies, forgive me," interrupted Amergin, "but what is this thing?" He gestured across the road.

"Oh, sorry, dear," replied Megan. "It's a crop circle. They've been turning up more and more often in recent years. Some of them are almost certainly hoaxes, people shuffling around in the dark with planks and bits of string, but some of them—I don't know. Some of them look too good to be fakes."

"I see." Amergin looked troubled. "And has anyone seen what creates these . . . these circles? Have there been any tales of lights or strange energies?"

"Well, there are reports of UFOs being seen near circles, you know, flying saucers?" Charly explained.

Amergin nodded.

Charly continued. "And people have reported radio waves and balls of light and all sorts of things inside the circles."

"This is grave," muttered the wizard, "grave indeed," and fell silent.

They ate their packed lunches there on the roadside, gazing out at the huge spiral stamped on the landscape. Then with reluctance they climbed back into the stuffy car.

⊹⊹⊹

"Yonder lies the Camp of Goosehill!" exclaimed Amergin, thrusting out one finger and knocking the rearview mirror out of alignment for the eighth time. "A fine town in its time, before the shadow of the Malifex fell upon it. It dates, you see"—he screwed himself round in his seat to address Charly—"from the days when the Malifex sought to speed the destruction of the Old Forest by teaching men the secrets of iron."

"Mmmm," sighed Charly, staring out of the window. "Nice." At first, she had been excited by Amergin's tales. They reminded her of that breathless summer with Sam, when they had battled the evil of the Malifex and her own powers had first begun to stir. But Goosehill was only the latest in a long series of hill forts, Roman villas, and ancient tombs that had attracted Amergin's eager interest since their journey had resumed after lunch. Now Charly just wanted the journey to be over. The holiday traffic was slow, and the sun beat down through the window. Charly continued to stare across the fields to the distant blue bulk of the South Downs, which had loomed on the horizon to their right for some time now. They reminded her of the ridge of hills behind their cottage, back at Woolgarston Farm, but these were much bigger and somehow more threatening. Their northern flank was scarred by deep clefts and gullies, like a row of clenched fists, and a dark blanket of trees clung to the steep slopes. Charly shivered and settled deeper into the back seat.

They followed the South Downs for much of the afternoon. Sometimes the downs were visible as a blue smudge on the southern horizon. Sometimes the road climbed their steep slopes or passed through them in cuttings through the blinding white chalk. They stopped once more, briefly, to buy gas and stretch their legs. Then it was back to the car and a long, dull crawl through the traffic jams on the outskirts of Eastbourne. As the afternoon wore on, Charly finally succumbed to boredom and drifted off to sleep.

✛

Sam carried his small traveling bag out to the car and dropped it into the open trunk. As he turned to go back into the house, he noticed a group of figures across the street, loitering by a phone booth. They were dressed all in black, long coats and leather jackets, dark hair, pale faces, nose rings, and pierced eyebrows. Sam paused. He had seen groups of Goths and bikers hanging around in town, but it was unusual to see them out here in the quiet suburbs. They were standing in silence, staring sullenly at the ground or out into space. But as Sam was about to turn away, one looked up, and their eyes met for a moment. Sam felt a shudder start at the base of his neck and run down through his shoulders. Turning quickly, he headed back into the house.

Ten minutes later, his father eased the car out of the driveway and turned left into the road, passing the phone booth. Slumped in the back seat, Sam gazed out of the window with a feeling of mild anxiety, but the group had vanished. He settled back and closed his eyes. As the car pulled away smoothly, a handful of dry leaves, ragged survivors of the previous autumn, swirled briefly into the air and danced along the pavement. As quickly as it had arisen, the vortex of air collapsed, and the leaves whispered to the ground once more.

✛

Charly awoke to find that they had arrived in Hastings. The car had slowed to a crawl in the holiday traffic pouring down into the town from the high ground to the north. Twisting her head from side to side to loosen the stiffness in her neck, she peered out of the window. The streets were teeming with holiday visitors, brightly colored hordes in T-shirts and shorts despite the weak spring sun. Tour buses were pouring out more of them every minute. The car reached the bottom of the long hill and crept around the corner onto the seafront. To her left, along a side street, Charly saw the cluster of strange buildings, narrow and dark, that loomed above the crowds. They looked like wooden sheds, painted a somber black, but they were three stories high, as if a collection of garden sheds had stretched upward to find the sun.

Megan, tired and irritable after the long journey, swerved out from behind a tour bus that had stopped to drop off its passengers and sped off along the seafront. Soon after, however, she turned inland again and slowed as the streets became narrow and choked with parked cars. The engine began to labor as they climbed back up the hill. Rounding the squat bulk of the church of Saint Clement, patron saint of fisherfolk, Megan turned into a tiny side street and pulled to a halt. Above them, sheltering under the bulk of West Hill, towered the faded paintwork of the Aphrodite Guest House. Leaving Amergin and Charly to struggle with their bags, Megan strode inside to find the landlady, Mrs. Powell.

"My dear!" cried Mrs. Powell as Megan entered.

"Hello, Mrs. P." replied Megan with a tired smile,

bending slightly to embrace the old woman.

"You look dreadful. Come on in. I'll put the kettle on." Mrs. Powell bustled off to the kitchen at the rear of the building, and Megan could hear the comforting clinks and clatters of tea being prepared.

As she wandered through to the kitchen in Mrs. Powell's wake, she heard the front door open and Amergin and Charly shuffle in with the luggage. She shouted, "This way!" over her shoulder and made her way to a battered old chair by the stove, where she collapsed with a sigh.

Charly burst in moments later and ran over to Mrs. Powell. Grabbing her in a boisterous bear hug, she shouted, "Hi, Mrs. P." and stepped back.

Mrs. Powell turned and fixed her with a penetrating stare from the palest of blue eyes, then broke into a grin. "My dear," she said, "I swear you're prettier than ever! And so tall!"

Charly was, in fact, about the average height for her age, but even so, the top of Mrs. Powell's head barely reached her chin. The old woman was dressed all in black—a long black skirt and a baggy black sweater with a large and saggy turtleneck. Like Megan, Mrs. Powell was a practicing Wiccan, but unlike Megan, she believed in looking the part. In addition to her preference for black, she was festooned with an assortment of beads, chains, and mystical amulets. Her hair was dyed an alarming shade of foxy red, fading to a line of gray at the roots. All in all, she looked as excitingly witchy as anyone Charly knew.

Mrs. Powell suddenly noticed Amergin, who was lurking by the kitchen door looking uncomfortable. She raised one eyebrow.

"Oh, sorry, yes," said Megan, "Mrs. P., this is Amergin. Amergin, Mrs. Powell."

"My dear lady," began Amergin, striding across the room with one hand extended, "delighted . . ." and then he faltered under the force of those piercing blue eyes.

"A pleasure, I'm sure," replied Mrs. P., shaking his hand as if it was a dead fish. "Megan has told me all about you."

Amergin gave her a nervous smile.

Mrs. P., her eyes never leaving Amergin's, said, "Well, you're very welcome in my house, Amergin." She turned to Megan, and the wizard visibly sagged with relief. "I've given you your usual rooms—first floor, with a view of the sea. Oh, my dear, it's super to see you again! I'll make a spot of dinner. No, I insist! Off you go! Freshen up! Come back down at six." And with that she began to clatter around the kitchen once more.

✦

Precisely at six, they assembled in the dining room, taking their places around a battered old table. Mrs. P. bustled around with steaming bowls of food before collapsing into her chair in a jangle of beads.

"So," she began, "Charly. Tell me, has your mother spoken to you about your initiation?"

"Mrs. P.," interrupted Megan, "it's a little early to be thinking about that. She's only—"

"Megan," said Mrs. P. sternly, "look at the child."

"What about it?" Charly looked from Mrs. P. to her mother, then back again.

Megan sighed, looking suddenly tired.

25

"I think it's time, my dear," said Mrs. P. "From what you tell me, she's had, shall we say, adventures already. Who knows what the future holds?"

"She's too young." Megan frowned down at her plate. "And besides, we've only just got here. There are preparations to be made, correct ways of doing things. We can't just rush into it."

"Flimflam," replied Mrs. P. "And you know it."

"If one of you doesn't tell me what you're talking about soon, I think I'm going to scream." Charly folded her arms and looked exasperated.

Mrs. P. looked from mother to daughter, marveling again at the similarity. "Have you been reading your books, my dear?" she asked.

Charly turned toward her. "Books? Oh, those books. Yes. I have my own *Book of Shadows*, and I've learned all the responses to the rituals. But . . ."

"Good," said the old woman decisively. "Eat up. I'll get my things together."

"You mean, I'm going to be initiated now?" asked Charly, grinning from ear to ear. "Cool!"

"We need to assemble a coven," Megan pointed out, "if we're going to do this properly."

"Not necessary," said Mrs. P. "We can do it just as well with three."

"I could help . . ." began Amergin.

"This," said Mrs. P. pointedly, "is women's business. Now come along. No time like the present."

◦┼◦

"Where are we going?" demanded Charly, struggling to keep up with Mrs. P. as she strode out of the house.

"The Firehills," the old woman called back over her shoulder. "It's a favorite place of mine for this sort of thing." She was carrying a large and mysteriously lumpy backpack and had a very businesslike air about her.

Charly looked to her mother but received only a rather worried smile.

They scrambled into Megan's car, and she raced off into the twilight, down to the seafront, past the net shops, and then climbing up once more, heading inland. Leaving the last houses behind, they emerged onto the windswept ridge high above town.

Under Mrs. P.'s direction, Megan parked the car at an overlook, and they clambered out. Off beyond the lights of Hastings, the sun was setting and air was growing cool. They crossed the narrow road and marched down a rough track that dwindled eventually to a footpath. Charly soon lost all sense of direction and concentrated instead on the retreating backs of her mother and Mrs. P. They passed under trees, slipping and stumbling in the shadows, and finally emerged onto a hillside. The trees gave way to scattered bushes of gorse, jet black in the fading light. At the foot of the slope, the gray of the wild grassland was replaced by a different color, a vast expanse of pearl, tinged with the last light of the dying sun: the sea. Charly could hear its voice against an unseen shore, the eternal sigh and hiss of the ocean.

Mrs. P. had stopped and was looking around. She walked a few steps and stopped once more.

"What is she doing?" Charly whispered to her mother.

"Looking for somewhere suitable," replied Megan.

"For the ritual?"

"Yes, dear. For the ritual."

"But don't we need a full coven for the Initiation Ritual?"

"Ideally, yes. As I tried to point out to her. But in exceptional circumstances, it can be performed with fewer. Fortunately, we have representatives of the three aspects of the Great Goddess—Mother, Maiden, and . . . Wise Woman."

"Crone," said Mrs. P., coming to join them. "Say it, I don't mind. I've worked long and hard to earn the right to be called crone, nothing to be ashamed of. Maiden, Mother, and Crone: the Three in One. And here is the perfect setting. These, my dear"—she gestured around them—"are the Firehills, a very special place."

"Why are they called that?" asked Charly.

"Well," replied the old woman, "one theory is that it's because of all the gorse." She pointed at the dark mounds of the bushes. "Nearly all year, they're covered in flowers, and it makes the place look like it's on fire. A very pretty theory, if a little fanciful."

"What's your theory?" Charly knew Mrs. P. too well to think she wouldn't have one.

"One of the ways of controlling scrub like this is to burn it every few years." She smiled. "I know, not as romantic, sorry. Come on."

✛✛

"We won't do it sky clad," said Mrs. P., taking her place, "it's a bit chilly."

Charly was relieved. Sky clad meant in the nude, and the evening was cool now that the sun was down. They had meditated for a while, each of them sitting with their own thoughts as the sun dropped into the sea out beyond Hastings. Now Mrs. P. had brought them together in a grassy clearing among the gorse bushes. The bright yellow flowers were still visible in the twilight, and their faint scent of coconut hung on the still air.

Mrs. P. took a wand from her backpack, a short length of wood bound with silver bands and with a piece of crystal at the end. Holding it before her, she walked clockwise around Charly and said:

Blessed be those within this circle;

Cleanse heart and mind,

That only truth be spoken,

Truth only be heard.

She fell silent for a space of thirteen heartbeats and then continued.

"A seeker is among us . . ." and here she spoke Charly's secret name, the name she had chosen for herself and by which she would be known within the ranks of her coven "proven by magic, who doth aspire to join with those who follow the way of the ancient craft."

The ritual took its course, the ancient words familiar to Charly from her studies. At the correct points, she gave the appropriate responses to Mrs. P.'s questions.

"Do you seek the Way

That stretches beyond Life and Death?"

"I do."

"Will you serve the Goddess
And reverence the God?"

"I will."

"Will you guard that which is shown you
From the unworthy?"

"I will."

Finally, Mrs. P. made the sign of the five-pointed pentacle with her wand and said, "In the name of the Lady and those covenanted to her, I place this threefold charge upon you: to know the Goddess and the God; to love the Goddess and Her Consort; and, through knowledge of the Way, to serve the Goddess and the Horned One. Do you"—and again she used Charly's secret name—"freely accept the charge?"

"I do."

"So be it. Blessed be and welcome, dear friend."

After Charly had embraced her mother and Mrs. P., she stepped back, grinning. "So, is that it, then?" she asked. "I'm initiated?"

Megan dabbed away a tear from the corner of her eye. "Yes, sweetie. You've taken your first step along the Path. I'm so proud—" Her voice broke and she looked away.

"Mu-um," sighed Charly, looking embarrassed.

"Come on," said Mrs. P. "We should be getting back. It's nearly dark, and your friend Sam will be arriving soon."

✛•✛

Closing the door of her room, Charly flopped down on the creaky old bed and threw open her case. Rummaging

30

frantically, she found her hairbrush and ran over to the mirror. A few minutes later, there was a knock on the door and her mother's voice shouted, "Charly! He's here!" Charly yanked open the door with surprising speed and looking slightly flushed, stumbled out. Megan looked her up and down. "Your hair looks nice," she said with one eyebrow raised.

"Mu-um!" groaned Charly, but one hand moved involuntarily to her newly plaited braid. Together, they clattered down the stairs and into the lobby.

"Sam!" cried Megan as she spied a familiar figure at the small reception desk. She gave him a peck on the cheek before turning to his father. "Paul. Good to see you again."

They shook hands, Sam's father glancing around sheepishly.

"Er, thanks for having him, Megan. Hope he won't be any trouble." He cast a sharp look in Sam's direction. "Look, I'd better be off. I'll pick him up on Monday, OK? Around seven?"

"That will be fine. We'll see you then."

With a look of obvious relief, Sam's father headed for the door. He liked Megan and Charly, but the whole subject of last year's holiday in Dorset made him intensely uncomfortable. Try as he might, he couldn't remember anything after the first couple of days. He and his wife had come to an unspoken agreement. The subject of Dorset was not discussed. Frowning, he jumped back into the car and drove away.

In the street outside the guesthouse, a dust devil sprang up. Candy wrappers and cigarette ends danced briefly in the air and then, as if invisible strings had been severed, dropped to the ground.

╺┼╸┼╸

"So," began Megan, "how are you?" She took a step back and looked Sam up and down. Sam, remembering her ability to read auras, felt nervous.

"Yes," he stammered, "good. I'm fine. How are you?" he finished with a forced smile.

"We're fine. Aren't we, Charly?"

Charly was lurking somewhere behind her mother and had turned slightly pink.

"Hi, Sam," she said, trying to look uninterested.

"Well," continued Megan, "you two must have a lot of catching up to do. I'll be off. I'll send Amergin down." And with that, she clattered back up the stairs.

Silence descended.

"So," began Charly after a while, "you're OK, then?"

"Mmm. Yeah. You?"

"Good."

Silence returned once more.

"Look," said Charly, "there's a little sort of lounge thing just over here. Let's go and sit in there. You can take your bag up to the room later." With that, she turned and marched off through a nearby doorway.

With a sigh, Sam put down his bag and followed.

He found Charly curled in an old armchair, a hideous thing with bowed wooden legs and tattered floral fabric. She had her mother's way of sitting, legs tucked beneath her, very self-contained and still. She watched him as he lowered himself gingerly onto a sagging sofa. To avoid her gaze, Sam looked around the room. The walls bore a bold floral pattern in gold and burgundy, though much of this was mercifully hidden by a mosaic of old prints in ill-matched frames. Local scenes rubbed shoulders with gilded paintings of saints and lurid pictures of women dancing in stone circles. Sam even saw the face of the Green Man, over in one corner, his ancient amber eyes gazing out from a mask of foliage.

When he looked back to Charly, she was still studying him.

"How are you really?" she asked. "You look . . . different."

Sam looked down at the violent colors of the carpet. When he looked up, there was a sad smile on his face.

"I think that's about the right word—*different*." He sighed. "I'm OK, really. It's just been a bit strange, adjusting."

"I can imagine."

"Can you?" Sam's eyes flashed. "Can you really?"

"OK! Don't get so worked up! Just trying to be sympathetic."

"Sorry." Sam looked sheepish. "How about you?"

"Oh, I'm fine. Very well, in fact." Charly smiled.

"What? Why are you looking so smug?"

"I've just been initiated."

Sam looked blank. "Oh. Initiated, huh? Well, that must be . . . nice."

"You haven't got a clue what that means, have you?" snapped Charly in irritation. "Sam, you're so lame sometimes!"

"Sorry," said Sam, looking bemused. "It's something

33

important, then?"

"Yes. It's the first step toward becoming a practicing Wiccan. I've had to study for ages, all the rituals and responses and things. It's not even supposed to have happened yet. I'm too young, really. But after what went on last year, with the Malifex and everything, Mrs. P. thought I ought to, well, jump ahead."

"Right." Sam nodded, trying to look suitably impressed. "Well, um, congratulations, then."

"Thank you."

Silence fell.

"How's Amergin?" asked Sam eventually.

"He's fine. He's settling in very well—almost too well."

"How do you mean?"

"He's, I dunno, not very 'wizardy' anymore."

"Is there such a word as wizardy?" Sam asked with a smile.

"Is now." Charly stuck her tongue out. "At first, Mum and he used to spend all their time talking about magic and history and folklore, but after a while, Amergin got more and more interested in, well, *modern* things. Television, mostly. Now he spends most of his time watching Star Trek and bouncing up and down on the couch."

Sam smiled at the mental image.

"It's not funny! He thinks most of what he sees is real. *Independence Day* was on the other week, you know, with the flying saucers invading Earth? He started running round collecting canned food and telling us to go down into the cellar!"

Sam started to giggle, and the door opened.

"Amergin!" he shouted, jumping to his feet.

"Sam, my boy!" replied the wizard, grabbing hold of him and thumping him vigorously on the back. They separated and stood for a moment, grinning foolishly at each other.

"You look well, my friend," said Amergin.

"You look . . . bigger," replied Sam. "Around the middle."

Amergin glanced down. "Hrrrmph, yes. Megan has been looking after me. Come. She told me to collect your luggage and show you to your room."

✛

The shopping mall was silent. The hordes of day-trippers had returned home, and those tourists who were staying in hotels and guesthouses had not yet emerged to begin their nightly round of pubs and clubs. In the yellow sodium glare of a streetlight, the litter swirled and danced for a moment, and there was Finnvarr, Lord of the Sidhe, striding through the still night. Behind him came the Lady Una, seeming to float on air as the train of her black wedding dress rustled through the discarded burger wrappers. They moved down a long aisle of empty shops, their reflections flickering and dancing in the blank windows, until they came to a bench. The group of black-clad figures barely looked up as they arrived, but their excited thoughts raced from mind to mind.

What news? demanded Finnvarr.

We have found him, my lord! Our agents tracked him down and followed him here.

Here? inquired Finnvarr in surprise. *He is here?*

Yes, my lord!

We followed him. He is here, in the town!

And you are sure he is the one?

Yes, my lord. He is only a boy by the reckoning of mortals, but the power is in him.

Then he has been delivered into our hands. Finnvarr allowed a look of satisfaction to register on his face. *We must ensure that he meets with . . . an accident. And then the final obstacle will have been removed from our path.*

⊹

Sam came down to supper later that evening and edged nervously into the room normally used for breakfast. Charly, Megan, and Amergin were already seated at the table, and the remarkable woman who had opened the front door to him earlier was bustling around, collecting food from a hatch in the wall.

"Ah, Sam!" she cried when she saw him. "My dear, do come in, do! Sit down, yes, just there. That's splendid!" She smacked down a plate of food in front of him. "Tuck in!" And with that she shuffled off to the kitchen.

Sam glanced over to Charly, who was staring down at his plate significantly and then back at him. She pulled her mouth down at the corners, her tongue protruding.

"Charly!" hissed Megan, "Behave!"

Sam took a mouthful of what he presumed was cabbage and realized what Charly's performance was trying to convey. The food was awful.

Swallowing with difficulty, he said, "So, what's the plan for the weekend?"

"Well," began Megan, "the Jack-in-the-Green Festival

isn't until Monday, so we have Saturday and Sunday to do whatever we want. It's up to you, whatever you want to do."

"Right, thanks," said Sam. "So, what happens at this festival, then?"

"I thought you lived near here?" Charly asked.

"It's more than an hour away!"

"Ignore her, dear," suggested Megan. "Jack-in-the-Green is another name for the Green Man. He has lots of names, Jack, Attis, Puck, the Horned God, even Robin Hood. Anyway, the festival takes place in the old castle, up on the cliffs above town. It celebrates the end of winter when Jack-in-the-Green, as a sort of nature spirit, is sacrificed to release the summer. The whole thing reaches a climax when the Green Man—Jack—makes his way up to the castle, accompanied by his bogies—"

"Urgh!"

"Sam! It's short for *bogeymen*. They're traditional figures who form part of the procession. They guard Jack and guide him. Some of them are dressed all in green, with leaves in their hair, and some are dressed as chimney sweeps. It was the sweeps who started the tradition, you see." Megan continued, "Anyway, at the climax, the Green Man is dismembered—"

"Uuurgh!" repeated Sam.

"—and the pieces of foliage are thrown to the crowd, to set free the summer. If you catch a piece, you're supposed to keep it and burn it on the first bonfire of autumn. But most important for us, there are stalls around the castle grounds, and we rent one every year to sell my pottery to unsuspecting tourists." Megan finished with a smile.

"Sounds like . . . fun," Sam finished lamely.

"I would have thought," said Charly with a wry face, "that you would be interested in anything to do with the Green Man, after what happened last year."

Sam glared at her. "Well, excuse me, but this isn't some sort of hobby." He stood up. "I think I'll turn in. I'll see you all at breakfast." With that, he strode from the room.

After a moment's silence, Charly said, "Don't look at me. I didn't mean anything."

"I know, dear," said her mother with a sigh. "Sam's obviously still affected by what he went through."

"There is something about him," mused Amergin. He glanced at Megan. "Something lingers . . ."

"I know what you mean. We'll see how he is tomorrow." Megan stood up. "Come on. We'd better turn in too."

╪

In his room, Sam sat on the single bed and stared out the window. The moon, close to full, rode high in a sky of patchy clouds, and its silver light danced on the sea far below. Looking along the coast, he could make out the silhouette of the pier, a dark stripe cutting through the moon's reflected path. Hearing an unearthly screech, he glanced up and saw a lone seagull returning to its roost on some high rooftop. Suddenly, he was suspended far above the town, riding the sea wind with the tang of salt in his nostrils. And with a shake of his head, he was back in his room, a slump-shouldered figure in a pool of moonlight. With a sigh, he fell back onto the threadbare quilt and closed his eyes.

chapter 2

The screaming of seagulls awoke Sam from an uneasy sleep. Hundreds of them appeared to be roosting outside his window. The day had dawned bright and clear, with the promise of sunshine. Sam washed and dressed quickly, eager for breakfast. Taking the stairs two at a time, he burst into the dining room to be met by Mrs. Powell, who was setting the tables. A couple Sam had not seen before were seated in the corner, chatting quietly.

"Merry meet, my dear," said Mrs. P., smiling up at him. Even at this early hour, her piercing eyes were rimmed with heavy purple eye shadow and thick mascara. "Sit down, do! The full works?"

Sam looked puzzled for a moment.

"Eggs, bacon, fried bread, mushrooms?"

"Oh, right. Yes please, Mrs. Powell."

"Call me Mrs. P., my dear—everybody does." And she wandered back into the kitchen. Sam gazed around the dining room, taking in the nicotine-stained ceiling and the threadbare carpet. The door behind him opened, and Sam turned around quickly, expecting Charly. He found himself staring into the cold, glassy eyes of a gentleman in a black suit. After a moment's confusion, Sam managed a weak smile, and the man grunted in return before taking himself off to a table in the corner.

After a minute or two, the dining room door opened once more and Charly came in, followed soon after by Megan and Amergin. Over tea and toast, they discussed the day ahead.

"I thought we could have a look at the museum out on Bohemia Road," began Megan. "It's supposed to have a very good display of Native American artifacts."

It slowly dawned on Amergin that Megan was waiting for a response.

"Ahh, yes," he began tentatively. "That sounds very . . . very . . . *interesting*. And I hear that on the seafront there is a miniature railway." He gave Megan a hopeful look.

"Amergin," she sighed. "A miniature railway? Really? You used to be so interested in folklore."

"I am, my dear, I am." He paused. "But I've never been on a miniature railway."

"What about our guest?" Megan turned her attention to Sam.

"Uh, sorry." Sam looked uncomfortable. "Not really into museums."

"Sam gets all twitchy if he has to learn anything," explained Charly.

Sam was about to protest, but Megan said with forced cheerfulness, "Fair enough. We're here to enjoy ourselves, after all."

"Why don't I show you around the town?" suggested Charly. "The old wrinklies can amuse themselves."

Sam began, "Well—"

"Good idea," Megan interrupted. "You two go off and have fun. I'll take Amergin for a donkey ride and some cotton candy." She favored the wizard with a particularly sour look. Sam didn't relish being in Amergin's shoes.

Mercifully, the silence was broken at that point by Mrs. P., who bustled in with Sam's breakfast and began to take orders from the others. Sam listened with interest as she greeted the sinister figure at the corner table. Pretending to take an interest in the decor of the room once more, he turned casually until he could watch out of the corner of his eye.

"Morning, Mr. Macmillan," chirped Mrs. P. The man replied, too softly for Sam to hear. He was hunch shouldered, his black suit rumpled up in folds behind his neck, and his jet-black hair was parted severely down the middle. He had plastered it down onto his scalp with some kind of hair oil, but two strands—one from either side—curled free onto his forehead. They made Sam think of horns. He was smiling to himself at this thought when he realized that Mr. Macmillan was staring back, glittering eyes like pebbles of jet beneath bushy eyebrows. Turning slightly pink, Sam looked away.

Charly chose that point to elbow him in the ribs, making him jump and gasp for breath. "Come on," she urged, "eat up. We've got places to go."

Sam noticed that she had opted for cereal and gazed down at his plate, where a barely cooked egg quivered in a sea of fat. He chased the food around for a few minutes and breathed a sigh of relief when Megan leaned forward and said softly, "It's OK. Leave it. I'll make excuses."

With a smile, Sam stood and followed Charly. Megan called after them, "Let's meet for lunch. How about fish and chips?"

With the memory of his abandoned breakfast fresh in his mind, Sam nodded vigorously.

"OK," agreed Charly. "What about the Mermaid? One o'clock?"

"We'll see you there," replied Megan. "Don't get into any trouble."

Sam and Charly looked at each other, shrugged, and hurried out into the spring sunshine.

┽┾

In a dead-end alleyway behind a row of shops, at the foot of a line of green plastic dumpsters, a single sheet of newspaper flopped and fluttered like an injured bird, though the day was still. It made a last lazy circle in the air and then, as if at the end of its strength, slumped to the ground. It came to rest against the toe of a black leather motorcycle boot. The rays of the morning sun glinted on a row of chrome buckles as the wearer of the boot kicked the newspaper away and strode out of the alley into the bustle of the street beyond.

From all over the town they came in silence, stepping out of alleys and doorways into the waking world. With pierced ears and dyed hair, leather and studs, the ancient host of the Sidhe took to the streets and caused no stir. To the tourists and townsfolk, they were one more thread in the tapestry of Hastings: bikers and Goths, morris dancers and New Age travelers. All the world seemed to converge on the town on May Bank Holiday. Old ladies sniffed and tutted at the piercings and peroxide and returned to their bingo games.

꘏

Charly and Sam clattered down the front steps of the Aphrodite Guest House and along a narrow path through the wild garden. A creaking iron gate opened out into a lane that led down steeply between two rows of tall houses. The blue sky was dotted with the white wings of seagulls. Their shrieking filled the air. Watching them, a frown crossed Sam's face, and he stopped for a moment.

"Are you OK?" asked Charly, looking back in concern.

"Hmmm? Oh, yeah. Fine," replied Sam. "Come on, show me the sights."

They passed the parish church of Saint Clement's, squat and sturdy, its tiny graveyard long since full. A neat fence held back a tide of buildings, red brick or black and white timbered, that peered down on the ancient grave-stones. Turning a corner, they emerged into High Street, quiet despite its name. The business of the town had moved away, down to the gift shops and arcades of the seafront, leaving behind bric-a-brac shops and restaurants. Charly dragged Sam to a shop that sold crystals and fossils, jabbering away and pointing out her favorite specimens in the window. After a while, it dawned on her that she was doing all the talking, and she stopped.

Fixing him with a steady look she had learned from her mother, Charly asked, "What is it?"

"Uh?" Sam snapped out of his daydream. "What?"

"'Uh?'" mimicked Charly. "You! That's what! You've got a face like a wet hen. What is it?"

"Nothing," replied Sam, irritated.

"Oh, yeah?" Charly raised one eyebrow.

"It's nothing. I'm fine."

"This is going to be a long, *long* weekend if all you're going to do is grunt."

"Look, just leave me alone, will you?" shouted Sam. He turned and stamped off down the sidewalk, then realized he had no idea where he was going. With a sheepish smile, he turned around. Charly was standing with her hands on her hips, one eyebrow still raised.

"Sorry?" tried Sam.

The eyebrow remained raised.

"That was a bit over the top, wasn't it?"

Charly nodded. "Come on." She took him by the elbow and led him across the street to a tiny park by the church. Sitting him down on a bench she said, "Right. Tell Charly all about it."

Sam smiled despite himself and sat down next to her. Leaning forward, hands clasped together, Sam tried to order his thoughts. He was no good at talking about his feelings and preferred to keep everything locked away inside. He was also very bad at talking to girls, though it somehow seemed easier with Charly.

"You know last year, when it was all over," he began, referring to his final battle with the Malifex, in the circle of Stonehenge, "and I came back to Woolgarston Farm?"

Charly merely nodded, giving him the space he needed.

"You were already there. But I left you in the woods. On Dartmoor."

Charly said nothing.

"How did you get back?"

Charly thought for a moment, then said, "A girl's got to have some secrets." It sounded lame, even to her.

Sam was quiet for a while. Then he said, "I knew you'd say something like that." He paused again. "I haven't—" His voice cracked, and he had to clear his throat. "I haven't been the same, since I got back."

Again, Charly left a silence for him to fill.

"He's still here, somewhere." Sam tapped one finger in the center of his forehead.

"The Green Man?"

Sam nodded. "He never quite went away. It's like . . . you know the feeling you sometimes get, like someone's watching you? And when you turn round, really quickly, you almost see who it is, but not quite? It's like that. It's as if he's behind me but *in my head*. Does that make any sense?" He turned sharply to Charly.

She nodded.

"And it makes me different," he finished.

They sat in silence again, apart from the unceasing cries of the gulls and the far-off bustle of the town.

"I'm having trouble at school," Sam continued. "They can tell that I'm different. They bullied me at first, but I scare them, and they leave me alone now."

"What about your games?" asked Charly. "You told me you used to swap computer games and stuff. What happened to that?"

Sam looked Charly in the eyes for several seconds, then said, "Do you think, after you have faced the Malifex and his servants and defeated them, that there is a single

45

game left worth playing?" He sounded suddenly very grown up, and Charly understood exactly what he meant by "different."

"I guess not," she replied sheepishly.

Sam stared at the ground for a moment, then turned to Charly with a tight smile. "Sorry, but you did ask."

"Mmmm, yes, I did, didn't I? Come on." Charly decided it was better to drop the subject and jumped to her feet. "Let's go and explore!"

Sam looked at her for a moment and then, with a tired smile, replied, "OK. Let's explore. Lead the way."

┽┽┼

Along the streets of the Old Town they came, in twos and threes, long overcoats trailing like black wings behind them. The ancient Sidhe, the Faery Folk, were gathering for the hunt.

Down on the seafront, the Lady Una sat on the wooden backrest of a bench near the boating lake, her booted feet placed demurely together on the seat. She had exchanged her black wedding dress for something more practical—a black leather motorbike jacket and a flowing, layered skirt of purple velvet. Her mane of black hair blew around her face in the cool breeze from the sea as she waited. Soon they came, fifteen or twenty of them, arriving in small groups, casually loitering around the bench in silence. When all were assembled, the Lady Una favored them with her characteristic smirk and jumped lightly from the bench. With a *click-click* of stiletto heels she paced off along the seafront, and her subjects followed behind.

⊹⊹⊹

"Wow!" exclaimed Sam, "It's heaving!"

They had left behind the relative quiet of High Street and plunged into the brightly colored chaos of holiday Hastings. The streets echoed to the rumble of powerful engines as bikers converged on the town. Over the years, the bikers had become a local tradition, and now hundreds of them paraded their machines along the promenade. The riders wove in and out of processions of buses pouring out their tourists. Here and there a knot of morris dancers in bells and ribbons pushed their way through the crowds, jingling and merry. The air was heavy with the smell of fried food and the salty tang of the sea. Sam found himself smiling, caught up, despite himself, in the holiday atmosphere.

"Come on!" shouted Charly. "This way." She plunged off across the road, dodging in and out of the slow-moving motorbikes. Sam did his best to follow.

Charly stood for a moment on the opposite pavement, watching impatiently as Sam tried to copy her dash through the traffic. He was right. He did seem different. Distracted, as if he was listening to something no one else could hear. Looking around, she noticed a group of strangely clad figures clustered around a bench. *Weirdos*, she thought, taking in the nose rings and dyed hair. A few kids in her school dressed like that, when they could get away with it. Loners, mostly. Quiet misfits who wrote poetry and pretended to dabble in the occult. Charly, as a newly initiated Wiccan, had a very low opinion of dabblers.

She looked back and found that Sam had made it across the road and was gazing around in a vaguely bemused sort of way. "Come *on*," she groaned. "You're so *slow!*" With that, she set off along a road bearing a signpost to the strangely named Rock-a-Nore. As she turned to go, she noticed that the Goths around the bench were also on the move. For no apparent reason, this made her feel uneasy.

"What are these, then?" asked Sam, who had appeared at her side. He pointed to the buildings around them. They were among the tall black sheds she had seen from the car when they first arrived.

"They're the net shops," replied Charly.

"Right." Sam nodded. "And that'll be . . . where you buy nets?"

"Close, Einstein, but you're guessing. They mostly sell fish from them now. But it used to be where the sailors stored things, fishing nets and stuff. They were only allowed so much space each, so they built upward."

Sam's eyes tracked up the face of the nearest net shop. Black-tarred planks loomed above him—three stories, each with a small door, the upper two opening out onto empty space. They seemed rather sinister, as if something were hidden behind the doors that shunned the daylight.

"Cheerful choice of color," he muttered to himself.

"Come on," said Charly once more and pulled him by the arm.

They made their way between the somber rows of huts, picking their way through piles of bright blue plastic net and coils of orange rope. Charly kept glancing behind them.

"You OK?" asked Sam.

"Mmmm," replied Charly. "Sam . . . ?"

"Yeah?"

"Do you know any Goths?"

"Goths?"

"Yes—you know, the vampire look? Black clothes, pale skin, bad taste in music?"

"I know what Goths are. We've got them at home. In fact, there were some hanging around our house when we set off yesterday. But no, I don't know any Goths. Why?"

"No reason. Come on."

She set off once more. Sam frowned at her back for a moment, then he called after her, "You are a strange girl, Charly!"

He hurried to catch up and found that they were on the beach. From the back of the net shops, the land dropped sharply to the sea. Here the fishing boats rested among rusting winches and old fish heads, as if a freak tide had left them stranded. They sat high on the beach, a row of compact, muscular vessels, their bright paintwork streaked with rust. Between them were scattered the hulks of ancient bulldozers, collapsed in the act of hauling the boats from the grasp of the sea.

"There's no harbor," explained Charly as they wandered between the ancient hulls, "so they use the bulldozers to winch the boats up onto the beach. Sweet, aren't they?"

Sam looked unconvinced.

"My favorite's called *Young Flying Fish*." She gestured over to a pug-nosed little craft hung with faded orange floats and topped off with a jaunty red and white life belt.

"Uh-oh."

"What is it?"

Charly looked suddenly anxious. "You know when I asked you about Goths?"

"Yes?"

"Well, don't look now, but there's a big gang of them, heading this way."

Sam turned. Striding through the old plastic fish crates came a group of dark figures led by a young woman in a leather jacket. She was stunning—delicate features, flawless skin, and a mane of dark hair that streamed out behind her as she walked. Heavy boots crunched on gravel as she and her companions made their way purposefully toward Sam and Charly.

"Look," began Sam, "I don't know what's going on here, but I think we should get going. Charly?"

But Charly had already disappeared around the planked belly of one of the boats. Sam hurried to follow. Behind him, he heard the slither of stones as the black-clad youths broke into a run.

Sam caught up with Charly at full tilt and grabbed her by the arm as he passed.

"Come on!" he bellowed. "Get us out of here!"

"This way!" Charly dodged left, into the maze of net shops, dragging Sam after her. Darting from side to side, she led him between the towering black sheds and out into the street. Looking back, Sam could see close to fifteen Goths thundering toward them. The girl was in the lead, a look of savage delight on her face.

"Ooops!" shouted Charly. "Trouble!"

Sam looked in the direction she indicated. Perhaps ten more Goths were headed their way from the town center. Charly grabbed Sam's arm and pulled him in the opposite direction, out along Rock-a-Nore Road.

"Have you got any money?" she shouted.

"A bit. Why?"

"We're going for a ride!"

Up ahead, Sam could see a narrow, sloping gully in the towering cliff face that formed the backdrop to the street. Nestled at the foot of this gully was what looked like the top half of a small blue-and-white streetcar. Sam was dragged through a gateway and up past a sign that said: East Hill Cliff Railway. Dodging in and out of a scattering of slowly moving tourists, Sam and Charly skidded to a halt at the end of a short line. In ones and twos, the people they had passed on their way in wandered up and joined the line behind them. And then the Goths appeared. They had slowed to a walk and took their place at the back of the line, unpleasantly close behind.

Charly risked a glance back and found herself looking into the baleful gaze of the girl in the leather jacket. Their eyes locked, and Charly's head began to spin. The girl smirked at her discomfort, and Charly felt a wave of anger sweep over her. She broke the eye contact and hissed at Sam, "Get your money ready."

Sam rooted around in his pocket and found enough change for the fare. They shuffled another place forward in the line. Ahead, Sam could see their transport—a small, squat vehicle, like a cable car. Unlike a cable car, however, it ran on rails that followed the steep slope cut into the cliff. The single carriage was rapidly filling up, and it looked as though only a handful of spaces were left.

At last, they reached the ticket office. "Two half fares, please," asked Sam.

"One of you will 'ave ter wait," said the man behind the counter. "Only one space left."

Charly went pale and glanced behind. A wave of malice washed over her again as she met the eyes of the dark-haired girl.

"But we're together," pleaded Sam. "Please?"

The man thought for a moment. "Oh, go on, then." He smiled. "Don't want ter stand in the way of young love."

Sam went pink, but he handed over his money with relief. Grabbing Charly's arm, he dragged her toward the carriage, and they piled inside. Squashed together in the sweaty throng of tourist bodies, they peered out through the glass as the Cliff Railway whisked them upward. Charly beamed down at the pale faces of the Goths and waved maliciously.

"Well," breathed Sam at last. "What do think that was all about?"

"You're asking me? I thought you might know."

"Nope. We'll have to ask Amergin."

The carriage finished its smooth ascent, and the doors opened. With relief, Charly and Sam spilled out into the fresh air and made their way out onto the grassy summit of East Hill.

"We'd better make our way back down fast," said Charly. "The next carriage load is probably on its way up by now."

"Do you think they'll follow us?" asked Sam.

"How should I know?" Charly exclaimed in exasperation. "I don't even know why they chased us in the first place. Although that girl . . ." her voice trailed off.

They followed a path across the brow of the hill, heading for the steep, meandering steps that led back down toward the Old Town. Sam paused, looking down at the sprawl of buildings far below, the tiny boats hauled up onto the beach, the shadowy towers of the net shops, and farther along the shore, the multicolored bustle of the town. He felt a sudden breeze and turned around.

An unseen force was lashing the short grass of the hilltop. Here and there, cigarette butts and discarded tickets swirled around in frantic spirals. Suddenly—and Sam at first doubted his own eyes—suddenly they were surrounded by the Goths who had pursued them from the beach. Arranged in a loose semicircle, the black-clad figures stood in silence, as if newly sprung from trapdoors in the grass.

Sam and Charly moved closer together. The girl in the leather jacket raised one hand, palm upward and fingers curled like claws. Once more the breeze sprang up, not swirling now but blowing steadily off the land and out to sea. Gradually, the breeze increased in strength, until Sam and Charly were buffeted by its force and had to lean forward into the gale to keep their balance.

Sam glanced behind at the dizzying drop down to Rock-a-Nore Road. The black-haired girl abruptly clenched her fist and brought her elbow sharply down by her side. A savage gust smashed into Charly and Sam, drawing tears from their eyes and making them stagger backward. Charly felt one foot slip on the grassy edge of the cliff and clutched at Sam's arm.

Sam glanced backward once more. "Charly," he hissed, "you're going to have to trust me now."

Charly gave him an uncomprehending look, then shrieked in terror as he launched himself backward into the void, dragging her after him.

⁘

And then, with a familiar swirling sensation in her mind, Charly felt the wind beneath her wings and screamed once more, this time with the high, plaintive cry of a gull. Together, she and Sam wheeled on the warm updraft from the sea, white wings flexing and rowing the air. Sam turned and plunged, and Charly followed him, down to a concealed yard behind a seafront café. Again, she felt the swirling sensation of dislocation, and she was back in her human form.

"Don't *do* that!" She laughed, exhilarated and relieved, slapping Sam on the arm.

"Sorry." He grinned back. "You OK?"

Charly nodded.

"Come on, then. We've got a lunch date."

⁘

They stepped out through a narrow passageway into the crowded streets and found themselves close to the Mermaid Restaurant. Megan and Amergin were already seated at a white plastic table, four steaming plates of fish and chips in front of them. With a wave, Charly and Sam made their way through the crowd and took their seats.

"Mum," began Charly, tucking into a chip, "you will never guess what just happened to us—are you two OK?" Charly sensed a certain coldness in the air.

"Oh, yes," replied Megan, "we've had a great time. We've been on the choo-choo train, haven't we?" She favored Amergin with a sour look.

"We can go to the museum this afternoon," said Amergin with the look of a man in the doghouse.

"Anyway, go on," continued Megan. "What happened?"

"We got chased by weirdos! We had to jump off the cliff!"

Megan looked shocked.

"It's OK. Sam turned us into gulls."

Megan looked only slightly less horrified. "Who was chasing you?" she demanded.

"Weirdos! Dressed in black, you know—Goths. There was this girl, and she made the wind start blowing. Nearly blew us off the cliff— "

"The wind?" snapped Amergin, suddenly alert. "You say she made the wind blow?"

"That's right," agreed Sam. "She lifted her hand up and the wind started blowing."

"Describe these . . . these Goths."

"Dressed all in black, pale faces, long hair, tall, and thin—Goths. You know." Charly shrugged.

"Ah," sighed Amergin. "This is grievous."

"Oh, dear," whispered Charly to Sam, "He's off again."

"What is it, Amergin?" asked Sam.

"There is one race, my friend," began Amergin, "who has the power to command the wind. The Hosts of the Air. They are known by some as the Faery Folk, by others—"

"Fairies!" spluttered Sam, almost choking on a chip. "These weren't fairies. No wings, for a start."

Amergin chose to ignore him. "They are an ancient race, cold and cruel. The Sidhe they were once, in ancient Ireland, and before that, the Tuatha de Danaan."

"I know that name," said Charly thoughtfully. "You've mentioned them before."

"Aye, child, for my path and theirs have crossed." Amergin fell silent, lost in thought.

"There's a story coming," Sam whispered to Charly. "Get comfortable." She kicked him under the table.

"Long ago," began Amergin, "as I have told, I came to the land you know as Ireland with my people, the Sons of Mil. And we saw that the land was fair and desired it. But a race dwelled there before us—the Children of the Goddess Dana, the Tuatha de Danaan."

"So what did you do?" asked Charly.

"We took their land from them," Amergin replied simply. "We slew them and took their land from them. And those we did not slay, we drove underground. Into the Hollow Hills."

"Where's that?" asked Sam.

"The Hollow Hills are . . ." Amergin trailed off. "Here . . . and not here."

"Right. That's cleared that up."

"Sam!" hissed Charly.

"The Hollow Hills," continued the wizard, glaring at Sam, "are a realm separate from ours, touching upon it in some places but in others far removed. There are gates, doorways into the hills, but once a man enters, he can never know where—or when—he will emerge."

"So," began Sam, "these fairies—the Sidhe—you and your tribe took their land from them, right?"

Amergin nodded.

"And you killed most of them and drove the rest underground somewhere?"

Amergin nodded again, looking unhappy.

"And you're the last survivor of the Milesians, the sons of Mil, yes?"

Another nod.

"So why are they chasing Charly and me? If they've got an axe to grind with anyone, shouldn't it be with you?"

"It may be," replied the wizard thoughtfully, "that they are trying to get to me through you."

"Well," said Charly, "could you arrange to have them chase you next time?"

"I think," replied Amergin, "'that we should all stay very close together for a while."

Their meal finished, they made their way back through the crowded streets toward the town center. Charly felt insecure, even in the presence of her mother and Amergin. The pavements seemed crammed with hostile faces.

Meandering through the streets of the Old Town, peering into the windows of old bookshops, they eventually spilled out onto the seafront once more, with its amusement arcades and souvenir shops. Caught up in the crowds, they walked on, under the foot of West Hill.

Above them loomed the ruins of the castle, where the festival would be held. It seemed to cling precariously to the rock, jagged and broken. Finally, they came to the newer part of town.

"I know," said Megan, pointing across the road, "let's go to the pier."

"I thought," replied Amergin rather huffily, "that you didn't approve of such things."

"It's industrial archaeology," said Megan, grinning, "a triumph of Victorian architecture."

They found a pedestrian crossing and shuffled with the crowd across the busy seafront. The pier launched itself out to sea from a wide plaza, ringed by stalls selling ice cream and seafood and dotted here and there with jugglers. Passing through a narrow gate, they found themselves out over the sea. The restless motion of the waves was visible through cracks in the old planks beneath their feet. They strolled on, with the sea breeze in their faces, past fortune-tellers and hot dog stands, past the old ballroom, to the farthest end of the pier. Here they stopped and leaned against the railings in a comfortable silence, gazing out to sea.

"I was thinking," said Charly after a while.

"Blimey!" said Sam, and there was a brief struggle as Charly attempted to throw him over the railing.

Eventually, she continued. "I was thinking, this is probably a bad place to be."

"In what way?" asked her mother.

"Well, we're right out here, in a kind of dead end. If the . . . What were they called?"

"The Sidhe," said a cold voice from behind her.

Simultaneously, Charly, Amergin, Sam, and Megan spun around. They found themselves face-to-face with the Host of the Sidhe, with Lord Finnvarr at their head. Strangely, though, it was Finnvarr who looked most surprised.

"You!" he cried, pointing at Amergin.

"My Lord Finnvarr," replied the wizard, inclining his head.

"But you should be dead!"

"It's a long story," replied Amergin.

The Lord of the Sidhe fell silent, but a mental argument raged between his mind and those of his lieutenants.

You said it was the boy! he raged.

That is what we believed, my lord. He has the power.

But the Bard, the destroyer of our people. . . . You fools! You pursue a child, while Amergin of Mil yet walks the earth? Take him!

But, my lord—

Take him!

Heavy boots thudded on the planking of the pier as two of the Sidhe strode forward. Amergin raised his hands and began to make a gesture of warding, but the air began to swirl around him. From his feet upward, he began to fray, his shape losing definition and shredding away into the vortex of air. Just before he vanished, he cried out, "Sam! The Hollow Hills!" And then he was gone.

chapter 3

Back in the Aphrodite Guest House, Megan sat in one of the old armchairs in the residents' lounge, lost in her thoughts, her face pale. Sam paced back and forth, unable to sit still, while Charly looked helplessly from one to the other. Somewhere, she could hear a clatter as Mrs. P. bustled around making tea. After a few minutes, she returned with a tray laden with cups and a steaming teapot. Settling into one of the remaining chairs, she looked at Megan and said, "So, my dear, what happened?"

Megan was silent for a moment. Then, "It was horrible. He just . . . sort of came apart. And then the rest of them, the Sidhe, they disappeared too. A little whirlwind, starting at their feet, and then they were gone. And last of all, that girl—"

"I told you about her, Mum. I hate her!"

"Now, now, dear," said Mrs. P. "Hate is a strong word. You say"—she returned to Megan—"that he spoke before he vanished?"

"The Hollow Hills," said Sam, looking up from the floor.

"The Hollow Hills?" Mrs. P. jumped to her feet. "Come on, darlings, follow me. And bring your tea."

With surprising speed, she led them up the stairs, past the guest rooms, to the highest landing of the house. Here she selected a key from the bunch that hung at her waist and opened the final door.

"Wow!" said Sam, following her into the room. Mrs. P.'s private quarters were in the attic of the old house, and the room they had entered—a kind of combined study and living room—had windows on three sides. The farthest, in the gable end, overlooked the sea. Light slanted in dusty columns and pooled on the floor—or what was visible of it.

"Sit yourselves down, dears!" called Mrs. P., bustling over to the bookshelves. She returned with an armful of books and plonked herself in a chair at one of the desks. Humming tunelessly, she leafed through several of the volumes, then cried, "Aha! Here we go!" She began to summarize the text in front of her. "The Sidhe—or Tuatha de Danaan—described in *The Book of Leinster* as 'gods and not gods' . . . blah, blah . . . *sidhe* is apparently also the Gaelic word for the wind . . . blah . . . here we go—

"'The Host of the Air' or 'The Host of the Hollow Hills,' the inhabitants of the 'Otherworld,' who roam the country four times a year, around the four great festivals: Samhain, Imbolc, Beltane, and Lammas. Well, there you have it." She looked at them over the top of the book. "Beltane is—or was—May Day. That's why they're around now."

"So," asked Charly, "what about these Hollow Hills?"

"Well," replied Mrs. P., "the Hollow Hills were once thought to be barrows—you know, burial chambers?"

Sam and Charly nodded. They were very familiar with barrows from their adventure the previous year in Dorset.

"But that word comes from the Old English word *beorh*, which makes no distinction between artificial mounds and natural hills. So there seems to be some confusion. It was once thought that tales of fairies taking people into the Hollow Hills referred to barrows, which are obviously hollow, because they're tombs, but this"—she tapped the page—"suggests that the ancient accounts might have been referring to actual hills—a kind of mystical Otherworld inside the hills of Britain. There's even a suggestion here that they might be bigger on the inside than they are on the outside, if you see what I mean."

"And what about the Sidhe?" asked Megan. "Is there any more information about them? We know where they came from, but who are they?"

"There are mentions of various kings of the Faery Folk, or the Gentry, as they are sometimes known. Where are we? Yes, here—the most powerful of the kings appears to be Finnbheara, or Finnvarr, of Cnoc Meadha in County Galway. His bride is the Lady Una—"

"That's her!" exclaimed Charly. "The girl in the leather jacket. That's her. I know it is!"

Mrs. P. looked over her book. "What makes you say that, dear?"

Charly frowned. "I don't know. I just . . . suddenly knew, when you said her name."

"Mmmmm . . . Anyway," continued Mrs. P., "the Tuatha de Danaan were defeated by the Milesians—that's Amergin's mob—and largely disappeared. But then they begin to crop up in legend; the Faery Folk, dwelling within hills from which music and feasting can be heard; traveling the land on horseback or in the form of whirlwinds. Apparently, when country folk see leaves whirling in the road, they still bless themselves, thinking that the Sidhe are passing by."

"So," sighed Megan, "it's clear what they want— revenge."

"If, as you tell me, Amergin is the last survivor of the Milesians, then yes," agreed the old woman. "It seems likely."

"I'm going to rescue him," said Sam, suddenly.

"No, you're not," replied Megan, just as quickly.

"Why not?"

"It's too dangerous."

"But I defeated the Malifex! How dangerous can it be?"

"Oooh!" exclaimed Charly. "Hark at Action Man!"

"We're talking about an entire race or what's left of them," agreed Megan.

"So what do we do?" demanded Sam. "Sit here and hope he gets out on his own?"

"But we don't even know where they've taken him," said Megan. "He could be anywhere." She looked close to tears.

"The Hollow Hills!" exclaimed Sam. "Where else are they going to take him? Mrs. P.?" He turned to the old woman. "Does it say how to get in?"

"Sorry, dear?" Mrs. P. looked up from her book.

"How to get into the Hollow Hills? Does it tell you in the book?"

Mrs. P. looked thoughtful. "There was something," she began and jumped up, returning to her bookshelves. "Where was it? Ah, yes . . . here. William Lambarde." She held up an ancient, leather-bound book. "A *Perambulation of Sussex*, published in 1578. I've always been intrigued by this. Where is it? Here we go." She cleared her throat and began to read aloud in strange, old-fashioned English:

"He who woulde be a Walker Betweene Worlds, and consorte with Fayries, must take hym to those hilles which men term Barowes, being hollowe, and knocke thrice, and the hill shall open unto hym. To the Wyse, these gaytes be signified by the elementes, being the Gates of Air, Fyre, Yerth, and Water."

There was silence.

Eventually, Sam said, "And that helps, does it?"

"It's a start," Mrs. P. replied with a sniff.

"What's *yerth?*" asked Charly.

"Earth, sweety," explained Mrs. P.

"So we just find a likely spot and knock three times, and they'll let us in?" demanded Sam.

"Not just any spot," said Megan patiently. "At one of the Gates, which seem to be associated with the four elements—earth, fire, water, and air. Anyway, you're not going, and that's that. I told your parents I'd look after you this weekend. And I will." She stood up. "Come on. There's no use moping around here. I'm sure Amergin will be fine. He's a powerful wizard."

"I'll go and start dinner," said Mrs. P. Sam groaned inwardly. "You'll feel more positive with something tasty inside you."

✛

They filed downstairs, Megan and Charly going to

their rooms, Sam and Mrs. P. continuing down to the ground floor. When Mrs. P. had shuffled off to the kitchen, Sam made his way to the residents' lounge. There, he rummaged around briefly in a pile of brochures and leaflets, pulled out a tattered, pink-covered map, and retired to a low coffee table.

Spreading the map out on the table, he began to scrutinize it, pushing down the stubborn folds. One index finger hunted here and there like a dog on a scent trail. To the north of the pink coastal sprawl of Hastings was the bewildering patchwork of the Weald, a green maze of tiny woods and narrow lanes. No use. No hills. Farther west, the bleak expanse of Pevensey Levels, crisscrossed by a thousand streams and ditches. Still no hill. And then the urban stain of Eastbourne, and just beyond, he found what he was seeking. On the western edge of the town, the South Downs began, a swirling thumbprint of contour lines and, dotted across them, the words he had hoped for: Long Barrow, Tumuli, Earthworks. The names brought a shiver. All his adventures had begun when Charly had told him of the barrow behind her house, high on Brenscombe Hill.

So, if it was barrows he wanted, then this was the place to start. He noted the name of the nearest village— Wilmington. Just then, somebody came silently into the room. Sam saw movement from the corner of his eye and jumped. It was Mr. Macmillan.

"Ah, good evening," he rasped, forcing a smile. "Poring over the map, are we?" He seemed suddenly very interested, peering down with his head on one side, attempting to read the inverted place names.

Sam began to fold the map up. "Just finished, actually," he said coldly, putting the map back with the brochures.

"Yes, well," said Mr. Macmillan awkwardly, "jolly good. I'll leave you to it." And with another unconvincing smile, he left.

Sam stared at the door for a while, unnerved by the stranger's visit, but soon his thoughts returned to his dilemma. He couldn't just sit back and leave Amergin to the mercy of the Sidhe. After all, what was the point in being a hero if you didn't . . . well, do heroic things? But what, exactly, was he to do in this particular situation? In the past, he'd usually had Amergin on hand to offer advice, except in his final battle against the Malifex. But now, starting from scratch with only Mrs. P.'s old books and the wizard's final cry to guide him . . . Well, he didn't feel particularly heroic. He was about to give up and go to his room when Charly appeared.

"Well?" she said, flopping down in an old armchair.

"Well what?"

"You're going to do it, right?"

"Do what?"

"That's what I like about you, your sparkling conversation. Rescue Amergin! You're going to rescue Amergin, aren't you?"

"Err . . ." Sam looked uncertain.

"Oh, come on! You know you are. What's the plan?"

Sam smiled. "Haven't really got one yet," he admitted.

"Business as usual, then." Charly grinned at him.

Sam made a face.

"We need to find a gate," said Charly decisively, "into the Hollow Hills. Where's the nearest barrow?"

"Wilmington."

"Sorry?"

"Wilmington. Start of the South Downs. Other side of Eastbourne." Sam looked smug.

"I'm impressed! You're getting good at this, nature boy." Charly jumped to her feet. "What are we waiting for, then? Let's go!"

"We can't just *go*." Sam sighed. "It's getting late. It'll be dark in a few hours."

"Never stopped us before. Go get some warmer clothes and meet me back here. Come on! Move it!"

Sam looked at the floor for a moment, then grinned up at Charly. "You're a very bad influence, you know that?" He scrambled to his feet.

"Yeah, and you love it!" Charly called after him as he headed for the stairs.

Ten minutes later, they let themselves quietly out of the front door and walked swiftly down the garden path. Charly had raided the kitchen on the way out, and they gulped down sandwiches as they walked. Just before the iron gate, they paused, and Charly turned to Sam. "Well," she asked, "how shall we travel?"

Sam looked thoughtful. "We need something fast, and we need to navigate. I know. Let's try this." He closed his eyes.

Charly concentrated. Since her own tentative experiment with shape-shifting, she had been intrigued by the idea. She tried desperately to memorize the sensation as the world seemed to shimmer and recede, and then all concentration was lost as she tumbled toward the ground. She gave a flick of her wings and saw the bricks of the path blur and drop away as she swooped high into the air. Ahead, she could see Sam, a dark-brown speck wheeling against the blue sky. His wings were incredibly long and narrow compared to the size of his body, a shape made with speed in mind. With dazzling agility, the two swifts chased each other around the chimneys of the guesthouse, screaming like the damned, and then with a flick of those rapier wings, Sam was off, arrowing into the west.

╅╈╅

They kept the sea to their left at first, arcing and swooping through the sky, reveling in the sensation of flight. The feeling of speed was breathtaking. It was quite unlike anything Charly had ever experienced before, and she wanted it, craved the power for her own. After a while, Sam tilted his wings and slid down a hill of air, heading inland. Charly followed and found that they were descending over the Pevensey Levels, a vast, flat expanse of grassland, carved into a checkerboard by countless waterways. They chased the reflection of the sun as it sparked and glittered in the ditches, skimming so low that their wing tips drew lines of ripples on the surface of the water. And then Sam wheeled to the south once more, leaving the Levels behind as he circled the hazy smudge of traffic fumes that marked the town of Eastbourne.

Dropping lower, they sped over rooftops and roads and saw, stretching out before them like a rumpled green carpet, the beginning of the Downs.

Sam spotted what he was seeking, descended farther, and circled twice, giving Charly a chance to catch up. Then, as they slowed and approached the ground, the world tumbled again, and Charly found herself in her own body once more. Breathless with excitement, she grinned at Sam. "You do know how to show a girl a good time!" she gasped.

Sam smiled back. "Come on," he replied. "This way."

They were in a field dotted with the lazy black-and-white shapes of cattle. Over to their left, behind an age-worn stone wall, were the ruins of an old priory. Sam led them to a fence, and they scrambled over.

"Wow!" exclaimed Charly, gesturing ahead. "Look at that!"

"Yeah," replied Sam casually, "cool, isn't he?"

Across the road, the bulk of the Downs rose up above the village, and on the slope, dazzling white against the green, was the carved outline of a man. He stood with his legs apart and his arms raised to shoulder height, and in each hand, he appeared to be holding a tall staff.

"Were you expecting this?" asked Charly.

"Well, it says 'Long Man' on the map," explained Sam. "And there was a leaflet about him back at Mrs. P.'s. Come on—that's Windover Hill. There are barrows and things all over the hilltop, up above him."

They crossed the narrow road and climbed a stile over a fence. A footpath, tightly hemmed between the road and the edge of a cornfield, led along the bottom of the hill before eventually swinging in a series of curves toward the slope that bore the chalk figure.

At the corner where the path left the road at right angles and headed off across the fields, they came upon a man, sitting on a grassy bank in the sun, biting into a huge sandwich. Two long walking sticks lay by his side.

"Art'noon," he said, around a mouthful of bread and cheese. "Off to look at the Green Man?"

Sam looked startled. "Why do you call him that?" he asked.

The man gave Sam a searching look. "Well," he drawled, in a thick accent that reminded Sam of Somerset or Cornwall, "'E's white now, see, that's account of 'im bein' made o' concrete. But 'e used to be made o' chalk. Cut inter the chalk of the 'ill, so ter speak. An' sometimes, see, the villagers 'ud forget to go an' cut un, an' 'e'd get overgrown. An' then they'd call un the Green Man."

"I see," Sam said thoughtfully. "Any idea who he's meant to be?"

"Well, 'e's like one o' they candles, see?"

"Er, no," replied Charly, "not really."

"One o' they pictures, looks like a candlestick, then—all of a sudden—ye sees it's two faces, two blokes lookin' at each other. Most folks, tourists an' the like"—he pulled a face—"sees a bloke 'oldin' two sticks. But there's some as sees a chap standin' in a doorway."

Charly and Sam both turned to look at the far-off figure. It was possible, thought Sam, that what he had taken to be two staffs or spears could be the uprights of a doorframe. He turned back to the stranger.

"And what do you think?" he asked.

"Me? I reckon 'e's a windsmith."

"A windsmith?" Charly frowned.

"Used to be a lot o' windmills round 'ere; still is one over by Polegate. Used ter be a lot o' call fer a man as could read the winds. Windsmith used ter go round, studyin' the wind, learnin' its ways, an' givin' advice to them as wanted ter build windmills. Could almost see the wind, some o' they old windsmiths."

"I see," said Sam, exchanging a glance with Charly that said, *Let's get out of here.* "Well, we better get going. Goodbye."

The stranger fixed Sam with an odd look, almost pleading. "Think on it, lad," he said. "A windsmith, a man as reads the wind or a man holdin' open a doorway. Think on it."

Charly pulled Sam away by the arm. "Come on," she hissed. "He's weird."

Sam stumbled after her, looking back over his shoulder at the figure on the bank. He had returned to his sandwich, all signs of his recent intensity vanished.

They continued along the track, warm now in the late afternoon sun. The pathway looped across the field in a wide curve, taking them far out of their way before swinging back to the foot of the carved figure.

"Come on," said Sam, "let's cut the corner off—it'll take forever otherwise." With that, he set off into the field of young barley.

"Walk in the tramlines, you idiot!" Charly shouted after him.

"Eh?" Sam looked puzzled.

"The tramlines—the tractor tracks!" Charly pointed down to the parallel strips of bare earth left by the wheels of the tractor that had sown the crop.

"Oh, right." Sam hopped sideways, looking embarrassed.

As they shuffled side by side through the knee-high barley, a thought occurred to Sam. He glanced back across the field and saw that the stranger had risen to his feet. Lost in the haze of distance, he seemed to be staring steadily back at Sam. In each hand he held a long staff.

"That's it!" exclaimed Sam.

Charly paused in her tramline and looked back at him. "What now?"

"What he was trying to tell us!"

"Come on, spill the beans. Time's passing."

"The gates into the Hollow Hills are linked to the elements, according to Mrs. P.'s book—earth, fire, air, and water. And here"—he gestured up at the hillside ahead— "we've got a windsmith, a man who studies the wind, OK? The air? Standing in a doorway."

"You mean . . . ?"

"Yup, I'm sure that's the Gate of Air, where the Long Man is standing. Come on!" Sam strode off toward the foot of the slope, the barley hissing against his pants as he walked.

"How are you going to open it?" Charly called after him.

"Well," Sam shouted back over his shoulder. "I could go up and knock three times, like it says in the book, but somehow I don't think that's how Amergin would do it. I think he'd be able to open it from here."

Sam stopped in his tramline and raised his arm, fingers splayed. "Let's see what I can do!" Eyes closed, he sent out his mind, probing the earth of the hillside. The short grass and the thin, chalky soil tasted familiar to him, comforting, like putting on a favorite sweater. He cast about, moving the focus of his consciousness upward, until he encountered the base of the Long Man. His mind shied away from something strange, alien. He rolled the new sensation around in his brain, getting to know it, letting it wash over him. And when he was comfortable with it, he thrust forward, searching for weaknesses. *Yes*, he thought to himself, *I see*. With a flick of his will, it was done.

Opening his eyes, he saw that a vertical line was shooting through the grass of the hillside, upward from the giant's feet. With a deep, subterranean rumbling and the sound of tearing roots, the earth began to part. But something was wrong. All around him, the air was starting to shimmer. The hairs on the back of his neck and arms stood up, and his head was buzzing, the pressure building.

"Charly, get back!" he shouted, and then there was a loud crack, close by. Looking up, he saw a sphere of intense violet light, hovering just above his head, rotating at incredible speed. With another sharp *snap*, three smaller spheres broke free from it and drifted off, coming to a halt several meters away. Blue white energy was crackling to the ground like miniature lightning. The barley around his feet began to sway. He was at the center of a vortex of energy. He could feel the currents racing around him, and there was a metallic tang of ozone in the air.

There was another crack, and each of the three smaller spheres spawned three offspring of its own. They in turn drifted away and took up their stations in the air, tethered to the ground by lightning.

Sam was swaying on his feet now, at the center of a radiating pattern of intense purple white light. He felt as if all the molecules in his body were under the influence of some alien gravity, a strange tide that sent them flowing in circles within him. His vision began to sparkle around the edges, narrowing gradually as though the world was receding. Just before he blacked out, he saw every stalk of barley in a circle around him suddenly soften like hot wax and droop to the ground. And then his mind fled.

He opened his eyes to find Charly shaking him. "Come on!" she said. "It's closing!"

Sam pushed himself up on his elbows. He was lying at the center of a perfect circle of fallen barley, every stem lying flat and neat. Around the perimeter, equally spaced, were three smaller circles. Beyond those, he could just make out others, decreasing in size as they spiraled away.

"Hurry!"

He looked in the direction Charly was pointing. In the hillside behind her, vast doors of white chalk stood open, monumental slabs of white rock fringed with the torn roots of grass. But already they were beginning to close. The ground vibrated beneath him as the doors swung through their slow arcs.

Scrambling to his feet, he shouted, "Come on, then!" and began to run. Charly set off after him. They were still some distance from the gateway, with a long slope of grassland between them and the lip of the opening. The doors were past the vertical now, their speed increasing as gravity took hold. It dawned on Sam that they were never going to make it, not at this speed. With his head down and his arms pistoning by his sides, he accelerated, his breath rasping in his throat.

Charly was dropping farther behind. Try as she might, she was not as fast as Sam, and it was clear that even he was not going to make it to the opening in time. The huge doors were nearly closed now, a gap of perhaps five meters between them. She was about to give up when Sam suddenly seemed to vanish. Then she spotted him, a small, brown shape against the green of the hillside. He had turned himself into a hare.

No, she gasped to herself, *Sam, no. I can't!* She tried to form the shape of a hare in her mind, to capture the particular feeling that accompanied transformation, but her thoughts were in chaos. The more frantic she became, the more impossible it was to hold a shape in her mind's eye.

Sam was close to the threshold, long ears pressed back along his spine and powerful hind legs pumping. The gap was only as wide as his human arms could have stretched now, but he was so near. With a final kick from his back feet, he launched himself through the closing gap. Skidding to a halt in the darkness, he heard a vast, hollow boom as the mighty doors slammed shut, and he thought, *Yes! Made it!* And then he realized Charly was still outside, and there was nothing he could do. If he tried to open the doors again, he risked triggering another discharge of energy like the one that had created the crop circle. He reverted to his human form and sagged back onto the dry dirt floor, eyes pressed tight against the darkness.

Outside, on the short-cropped turf of the hillside, Charly buried her face in her hands, gave in to the frustration and the anger, and let the tears come.

chapter 4

Amergin struggled to raise his chin from his chest; a face swam into focus before him—high cheekbones, pale, flawless skin.

He's awake. Amergin heard the voice in his mind. The face withdrew into the gray blur.

Amergin mac Mil, came a deeper voice. *I am most surprised to see you again. And little has surprised me for centuries.*

The wizard raised his head once more and tried to focus. Off in the gloom, he could make out, with difficulty, a seated figure. "Finnvarr?" he croaked.

Aye, Finnbheara, Lord of the Sidhe, came a lighter voice, high and proud in Amergin's head. A figure broke free of the shadows and came toward him. The clicking of footsteps echoed off unseen walls. A pale face framed in dark hair loomed into his field of vision. *You look tired, old man.*

"And the Lady Una." Amergin sighed. "Lovely as ever."

Amergin, old friend, continued the voice of the Lord of the Sidhe. *Leaving aside the riddle of how you come to be here, alive, so many long years after you stole my country and butchered my people—*

"Ah," said Amergin, "you remembered."

You may be able to help us with another puzzle. We have recently noted that there is a power abroad in the land. The Old Ways crackle with it and overflow. It is as if the snows of a thousand winters have thawed, and the meltwater is come to burst the banks of the streams and ditches that men make. Why should this be?

"The Malifex," replied Amergin. "He was defeated, dispersed. His power is spread throughout the land."

Ah, said Finnvarr, *that one. I see a great tale waits to be told. You will tell it to us, later.* The Lord of the Sidhe shifted forward in his seat. *We would have his power, old friend. We would make it our own. And then no longer would we skulk in the Hills. We would reclaim the land that your people stole from us. Aye, and more. But something stops us. The power that opposed the Malifex, the Old One, Attis, the Green Man—something of him also remains?*

Amergin remained silent.

If my lord were to think that you were withholding something, said the Lady Una, peering once more into Amergin's face, *it would go ill with you.*

The wizard stared back into her deep black eyes for a moment and said, "My lady, I am the last survivor in this world of the race that destroyed your people and stole your land. I fear it will go ill with me whatever happens."

The Lady Una threw back her head and laughed.

⊹⊹⊹

High on the flank of Windover Hill, Charly sat with her arms around her knees and gazed out over the valley. The sun was low in the sky now, throwing a soft, golden haze across the air. Below her, the pattern of crop circles that had formed around Sam was stamped onto the landscape as a reminder of her failure. Her vision blurred once more. She blinked away the tears, then wiped her nose on the back of her hand. *It's not fair,* she thought. If she had Sam's power, she would revel in it, use it to its full, do good works with it. Not like him. *He's such a . . . such a boy!* she thought. And she just trailed in his wake, blown along against her will, being turned into things when it suited him. Well, she was a fully initiated Wiccan now. It was time she took charge of her own destiny. She scrubbed at her eyes and stood up. *Right. When brute force fails, it's time for female brain power.*

She turned and examined the figure of the Long Man, spread-eagled against the green hillside, but there was no sign of the doorway. The edges of the great slabs had merged back into the turf. If she couldn't follow Sam, she needed to get back home and decide what to do next. She'd done it once before. The previous year, when Sam left her to pursue the Malifex, she had made her own way home. No reason why she shouldn't be able to do it again.

Closing her eyes, Charly concentrated on a shape. She chose the swift once more; its feel was fresh in her memory. That previous time—last year in the woods on Dartmoor, when she had taken the shape of a flycatcher—it had helped to spin. She began to rotate on the spot, arms held straight out at shoulder height. Eyes tightly closed, she concentrated on the shape and feel of the bird. Nothing.

Feeling rather ridiculous—and more than a little

dizzy—Charly sat back down on the grass. She pulled her braid from behind her neck and fiddled with the band of elasticized fabric that held the auburn hair in check. Then she jumped to her feet again.

"Got it!" she exclaimed, out loud, and set off down the slope.

Taking up position in the center of the biggest crop circle, she held her arms out once more and felt the faint, leftover prickle of power radiating from the fallen stems. She began to spin, and moments later, a swift flicked its long wings and with a scream headed eastward.

✛

It took a while for Sam's eyes to grow accustomed to the dark. As he lay there in the black void, he thought, *This is it. She's going to kill me. There's no way she's ever going to forgive me for this one.* He sighed. Why couldn't Charly have just kept up? She made everything so complicated, typical girl. Oh, well. He was almost certainly better off without her. But he was going to be in so much trouble when he saw her again.

Sam scrambled to his feet and looked around. The darkness was not complete. Here and there, small cracks in the ceiling and walls let in narrow beams of light, swirling with dust motes. His night vision had been unnaturally good since his encounter with the Green Man, and he found that he could see quite well.

He was in a long chamber with an arched roof, presumably corresponding to the interior of Windover Hill. He turned to his left, hoping that this would take him roughly back in the direction of Hastings, though Mrs. P. had given him the impression that directions inside the Hollow Hills didn't necessarily match those outside. Still, he had to go one way or the other, and left would do.

The floor was dust-dry and chalky; clouds of white powder kicked up around his feet in the occasional shafts of daylight. The chamber gradually narrowed, the walls drew closer together, and the roof crept lower, until Sam found himself at a dark archway. From here, rough steps led downward in a tight spiral. Sam walked with the tips of his fingers trailing along one wall. The light was too faint even for his eyes. When he reached the bottom, the floor took him by surprise, and he stumbled. Opening his eyes, he found that he had emerged into a vast tunnel that disappeared into gloom in either direction.

The spiral staircase had taken away his sense of direction completely, so Sam chose left once more. Close to the foot of the stairs, the floor was uneven and rocky, but as he moved out into the huge chamber, it became smooth and well-worn, as if by the passage of many feet. Keeping to the center, where the floor was smoothest, Sam made good progress. After half an hour, he was sweaty and covered in dust, but he felt as if he had put some distance behind him.

The chamber twisted and snaked, so that the farther reaches were always out of sight, around a bend or lost in darkness. Otherwise, his surroundings seemed to change very little. In fact, Sam's progress was so monotonous that the sound must have been audible for several minutes before he noticed it. He heard a dull rumble, made indistinct by the echo of the high roof but drawing nearer. Sam stopped and looked around, but there was nothing to see in the gloom.

The light in the chamber was faint, rare shafts lancing down from the recesses of the roof far above, fading long before they reached the ground. Away from the central path was a jumbled chaos of boulders and slabs, a fragmented landscape of shadows and harsh angles. Sam could feel the vibration now through the soles of his feet and looked around for a hiding place.

At that moment, he saw motion to his right. Out of the darkness came figures on horseback, five or six of them riding in close formation. Horsemen of the Sidhe, black hair streaming out behind them. Their horses' hooves thundered on the hard-packed earth of the cavern floor, and the echoes boomed around Sam. Frantically, he looked for cover. He began to run, pounding along the path, peering into the pools of shadow between the great boulders, seeking an exit.

The riders were close behind him now. He glanced over his shoulder and saw the leader, tall and pale, bearing down upon him. His horse was as black as night, and fire flickered in its nostrils. Without a word, the riders hauled on their reins and brought their mounts skidding to a halt, clouds of dust billowing around their hoofs.

Sam darted off the path and began to scramble among the boulders. Behind him, in the silence, he heard a solid *thud* as a pair of leather boots impacted the ground. The lead rider strode toward him, confident, unhurried. Sam forced himself between two great slabs, ducked beneath a third and, on hands and knees, scuttled through the dust.

The ground was sloping upward now, ever steeper. Pushing through a final gap, he came up against the wall of the tunnel. Turning, he flailed with his legs, kicking himself backward until he felt solid rock against his spine. He thought about changing shape and tried to picture something—a bird, a mouse, anything—but in his panic no clear shape would form in his mind. He stared at the gap in front of him, panting in desperation, waiting for the inevitable pale face to appear. *I need a doorway,* he thought. *Why is there never a doorway?* He cast his mind out into the rock behind him, straining for that alien strangeness he had tasted in the Long Man gateway, the Door of Air. And fell, tumbling over backward. Light flashed before his closed eyes—on, off, on, off—as, head over heels, he rolled down a long slope. With a crash that knocked the air from his lungs, he came to rest in a tangled heap against a thorn bush.

⁍⁌

Charly reverted to her human form a short distance above the garden of the Aphrodite Guest House and skidded across the lawn. *I must work on my landings,* she thought as she came to a halt in the shrubbery. She scrambled up and brushed the dead grass from her clothes, then headed indoors.

Her mother was frantic. She jumped up from a chair in the residents' lounge at the sound of the door and ran out into the lobby.

"Where have you *been?*" she roared, "I've been worried sick!"

Mrs. P. emerged from the kitchen, drying her hands on a tea towel, and stood in silence, staring at Charly.

"Mum!" she began, "I'm OK. Don't fuss—"

"Don't fuss! I've—"

"I've been with Sam. We went to rescue Amergin."

"You went . . . oh, terrific." Megan raised her eyes to the ceiling. "So where are they?"

"Erm," began Charly, "there was a bit of a problem."

"Megan, Charly," interrupted Mrs. P., "I think we should go and sit down, and you can tell us what happened." She ushered Charly through into the lounge. Megan ran one hand distractedly across her face, then followed.

᛭᛭᛭

Five minutes later, Charly had finished her story. Silence fell. Eventually, Megan said, "What am I going to tell his parents?"

Charly stared at the floor.

"I don't believe this is happening," Megan continued. "At least, Amergin is an adult—there's a chance he can look after himself. But Sam . . . ? How could you be so stupid?" She gave Charly a despairing look. Charly felt tears spring to her eyes once more.

"Megan, dear," pleaded Mrs. P., "don't be too harsh on the child."

"I'm going to my room. I need to think." Megan stood up. "You, young lady, are so grounded—" She paused, then turned and marched out of the room.

Mrs. P. stared at Charly for a long moment. "Foolish and headstrong," she said. "And utterly reckless."

Charly screwed up her eyes and tried not to sob.

"And you're not much better," continued Mrs. P.

"Huh?" Charly looked up.

Mrs. P. was smiling. "Your mother, dear," she continued. "She was just like you, when she was your age. But not quite so talented. Don't take it too hard—she's upset and frantic with worry. I'll go and speak to her soon, see if we can come up with a plan. You go up to your room, and try to get some rest."

Charly nodded, wiped her nose on her sleeve, and headed for the stairs.

┽┾

Sam scrambled to his feet, ready to run. He was on a grassy slope, dotted here and there with scrub. A featureless sweep of grass stretched before him up to a clear blue sky. He walked up the slope a short way, but the turf was unmarked, featureless, apart from a scatter of dry sheep dung. It seemed unlikely that elves or fairies were going to burst out of the ground.

He turned around, and his eyes widened. The ground dropped away steeply, the scrub growing thicker toward the foot of the slope and merging into the fringes of woodland. A woodland that rolled away in all directions, a dense green rug thrown across the landscape, fading to the palest blue haze on the distant horizon. Here and there, a faint plume of smoke rose from a clearing, marking a hidden farm or village. But otherwise the trees had dominion, an ancient forest like nothing Sam had ever seen.

Well, he thought to himself, *no sign of Hastings.*

One of the plumes of smoke was close, no more than an hour's walk, Sam guessed. With no better plan, he descended the slope, scrambled over a rough hurdle fence, and set off into the trees.

From his view on the hillside, Sam had been expecting some sort of primeval wildwood, a tangle of thorns and brambles, but the forest was surprisingly open. Many of the trees had been cut at the base and left to regrow, craggy old stumps of hazel and hornbeam sprouting crops of tall, straight shoots, leaves fluttering like flags in the breeze. Here and there, a mighty oak or ash had been left to grow tall, great timber trees standing like pillars with their crowns in the sunlight.

Sam soon picked up a rough path that meandered between low banks studded with wildflowers. It was blue-bell time, and the ground to either side of the path glowed beneath a blue haze. The air was heavy with the perfume of a million nodding blooms.

As he walked, he became more than usually aware of the presence that always seemed to lurk behind his mind, peering through his eyes. The spirit of the Green Man within him recognized this place. It was the world where he had been born, the ancient wildwood where he had grown and flourished before humans, spurred on by the whispers of the Malifex, had destroyed it. The spirit seemed to push forward, until Sam felt as if someone were standing very close behind him, so close that if he turned and looked, they would be eye to eye. He heard, or felt, a chuckle—a deep current of mirth running through his head. Beneath the laughter was something wild, primeval, the music of pipes and the distant sound of horns.

Sam broke into a run, flickering through the shafts of light that pierced the high canopy. The fierce happiness of the Green Man swept over him, and he began to shift from one shape to another for the simple joy of it. He was a hare once more, a wolf, a polecat arcing through the long grass like a coiled spring.

Once he heard a snorting and rustling and feared that the Sidhe had returned. But it was only a herd of pigs, rooting beneath the oaks. They were leaner and hairier than the fat, pink animals Sam was used to, with a half-wild look to them. They ignored Sam, seeing only a young stag, and he moved on.

He passed a fallen tree, a giant of the canopy that had succumbed to gales or rot and had crashed down into the undergrowth. Its roots had taken with them a huge disk of earth, which stood now vertical, leaving behind a circular crater. The rain had filled it, and the creatures of the forest were busy claiming this new pond as their own. Yellow irises flowered around the edge, and kingcups, and the blue needles of damselflies darted through the rushes.

In a grassy clearing, Sam stopped before an area trampled to mud by deer and assumed his human shape. A huge butterfly, dark except for a lightning-flash of white across its wings, fluttered up from a hoofprint. Its wings glinted an intense metallic purple as it passed through a shaft of sunlight, heading up to the high canopy of oaks.

Sam was getting hungry. He had lost all track of time, but it felt like several hours since his last meal. He stopped for a breather, climbing the low bank and settling with his back against a tree. He sat listening to the sound of bird-song for a while, watching midges weave a ball of silver in the light that fell on the path below. And then, with nothing else to do, he continued on.

Soon he came to a patch of woodland that had recently been cut—the word *coppiced* sprang to his mind, though he wasn't entirely sure what it meant. Here the old stumps that he had seen throughout the forest had had their crop of tall stems removed, and piles of long poles were neatly stacked by the path. The great timber trees had been left to grow on and stood in majestic isolation in the wide clearing. Sawdust and wood chips littered the ground, but already primroses and purple orchids had pushed up through, basking in the unexpected flood of light that now bathed the forest floor.

A little farther on, Sam came across a series of low mounds. They reminded him of barrows or tumuli, but the earth was raw and fresh, and each was crowned with a wooden peg surrounded by turf. A wisp of smoke drifted from around one of the pegs. Sam went over to investigate. He placed one hand on the bare clay of the mound and found that it was warm. Moving on, he soon found an explanation for the mounds. They were charcoal kilns—the last in the line had been broken open and its contents removed. Glossy black charcoal was strewn across the trampled ground, and a pile of blackened logs stood to one side. He kicked at the scraps of charcoal, and they tinkled like glass. The trail of footprints and black dust led off through the trees, and Sam's eyes, following the trail, made out the dark shapes of buildings in the distance.

Sam edged into the clearing, eyes darting back and forth. A regular metallic ringing came from the largest building, as did the plume of smoke that he had seen from the hillside. The buildings themselves confirmed his suspicion. This was not his own time. Thatched and timber-framed, the sides daubed with mud and straw, these were no buildings from Sam's world.

There were three main structures: the largest in front of him, across a yard of bare earth, and two smaller ones—barns or storehouses of some sort—to either side. A few hens scratched around in the dust. The trail of charcoal fragments led to a neatly stacked pile of black logs by the main building. The metallic sound of hammering suddenly ceased, and a figure appeared at the door of the building ahead, a huge hulk of a man. He stared at Sam for a few moments, then beckoned, turned, and disappeared back inside.

Sam stood on the edge of the yard, paralyzed with indecision. The man had not seemed hostile. Otherwise, surely, he would have approached Sam instead of turning back. But was it safe to follow? Sam considered his options. He had clearly emerged from the Hollow Hills far from his own time. He was alone, with no idea of where or when he was or how to return. What did he have to lose? With a shrug, he set off across the yard.

It took a few moments for his eyes to adjust to the gloom. The windows were tiny, and the main source of illumination was a roaring fire in the center of the room. Silhouetted against its light was the bulk of the man who had beckoned. He had his back to Sam and was examining something intently.

"Welcome, lad," he rumbled, without turning around. His accent was thick but somehow familiar. "Don't 'ee 'ang on the threshold. Come on in."

Sam realized that he spoke like the man they had met at the foot of Windover Hill, who had told them of the windsmith. He stepped forward.

The man turned suddenly, and Sam saw that he was holding a long, curved blade. In a panic, Sam scuttled backward and collided with the doorframe, bringing down a shower of dust from the thatch.

"Oh, don't 'ee mind this," said the man, waving the blade at Sam. "New scythe blade; old 'un's as sharp as I am." He placed it carefully on a low wooden table.

"Run on an' get us summin' t'eat," he commanded. Sam was confused for a moment, but then a small shadow detached itself from the larger gloom and scurried past him. It was a young boy, covered in soot. Sam had a glimpse of wide, white eyes, and then he was gone.

"Don' get many strangers," said the man, folding his arms across his massive chest. He was wearing a long leather apron over rough brown leggings. His arms were bare and hugely muscled.

"I'm, er, lost," said Sam.

"I should say y'are," agreed the man, "a tidy way lost, an' all. A young 'un, too, ter be wanderin' the 'ollow 'ills."

"You know about the Hollow Hills?" Sam asked in surprise.

"Course I do, boy! I ain't no gowk! An' I knows a Walker when I sees one."

"A walker?"

"A Walker Between Worlds. One as uses the 'ills to get about, an' 'as commerce with the Faery Folk."

"I dunno about *commerce*," replied Sam. "I was trying to get away from them. They've kidnapped my friend."

"Ah, a sorry tale," said the man with a sigh. "Not wise to cross 'em, the Farisees. What did 'e do, this friend of yourn?"

"He invaded their land, killed quite a few of them, drove the rest underground."

"Ah. 'E'll be a pop'lar lad, then."

At that moment, the boy returned with wooden plates bearing thick slabs of coarse bread and slices of tangy cheese.

"Tuck in, lad," said the man.

"Thanks. I'm Sam, by the way."

"'Ow do, Sam? You can call me Wayland."

Silence fell as they applied themselves to the food. Eventually, Wayland said, "Youm gonna rescue 'im, then? This friend of yourn?"

"That was the idea," admitted Sam, "but I didn't get very far. I'd just found a way into the Hollow Hills when the Sidhe turned up, and then somehow I sort of fell out and ended up on a hillside not far from here."

"Aye, well, them as goes crawling round in the earth like moldywarps is arskin' fer bother."

"Moldywarps?" spluttered Sam, spraying crumbs.

"Little gennlemen in black velvet, as digs in the earth. Leaves their little mounds o' muck hither and yon."

"Ah, moles," said Sam and returned to his sandwich.

Wayland was quiet once more, chewing steadily. His face was weather-beaten and ruddy, like old leather, polished and oiled; and his graying hair was square-cut at the shoulders. His blue eyes twinkled in nets of fine lines as he watched Sam.

"Iron," he said, after a while. "That's yer lad for the Faery Folk. Iron."

Sam looked blank.

"Can't stand it, see?" Wayland continued. "Takes away their power, only thing as can kill 'em. You needs you some iron."

"Have you got anything I could use?" asked Sam.

Wayland dissolved into laughter. It went on for what seemed like an unreasonable length of time, and Sam was starting to look around in embarrassment when Wayland took a shuddering breath, wiped his eyes, and said, "'Ave I got any iron? I'm a blacksmith, boy! I've got precious little *but* iron! Tell 'ee what, you an' me, we'll make somethin', a good ole pigsticker fer visitin' bother on the Farisees!" The smith jumped to his feet. "Don't just sit sowing gape seed, lad. Tackle-to!"

┼┼┼

Charly lay on her back on her bed, staring at the ceiling. Her mother had gone upstairs with Mrs. P., up into the attic room, where they were now deep in discussion.

Closing her eyes, she pictured once more the crop circle forming around Sam, the spheres of light crackling and dancing, the breathtaking pattern of swirls stamped across the landscape. How typical of Sam, she thought. Miracles and wonders followed him wherever he went, and he blundered around in the middle of them, moaning and sulking like a child. He was a hero, yes. He had defeated the

Malifex, after all—but almost by accident. She had done most of the real work. And Amergin, of course. She sighed. It all came down to power again. Sam was a boy and had it; she was a girl and didn't. If only there was some way. . . . She thought again about her initiation and the books she had read as part of her training. Her *Book of Shadows* was full of tantalizing hints and rumors of the powers she would gain as she completed her training. One ritual in particular had always stuck in her mind, because it summed up the glamour of Wicca. It was central to the Craft and was carried out by the high priestess. Charly shivered just thinking about it. From her earliest memories, she had dreamed of one day becoming a high priestess, with her own coven.

An idea came to her and she sat up.

Her mother would go crazy. She felt sick when she thought of how mad her mother would be. But then she thought of Amergin and Sam and of how she had encouraged Sam to set off on his rescue mission.

Her mind was made up. She jumped off the bed and ran over to the window. The sun was setting off along the coast, its light glinting on the sea far below. Charly threw open the window and breathed in the salt tang of the air. Closing her eyes, she concentrated on a shape. It was becoming easier with every attempt. Moments later, a seagull flicked its white wings and headed into the east.

chapter 5

The sixty-five ships of the Milesians rode the swell off the coast of the new land, their tattered sails furled now. Amergin stood in the prow of the leading ship, one foot braced against the gunwale, and looked out over the expanse of green. As his eyes took in the rolling hills where the cloud shadows raced, his heart felt as though it would burst with joy. A song came to him—

Amergin. I know you can hear me.

An insistent pressure pushed against the edges of his mind. *Go away,* he thought, *this land is ours.*

Amergin. Stop it, now. You're wasting your time.

Again, the pressure, making colored lights dance behind his eyes. And then a searing pain that brought him gasping into consciousness.

That's better, said the Lady Una. *You can't hide in your memories forever.*

"My lady," croaked the wizard. He had neither eaten nor drunk for many hours now, perhaps days. It was impossible to tell in the darkness of the cavern. He peered down at the ghostly oval of Una's face, floating in the gloom below him. He was suspended in midair, far above the floor of the chamber, by a webwork of pale blue energy that crawled and writhed over his skin. His arms and legs were flung wide, and the pain in his joints was becoming unbearable. He was kept aloft by the will of a circle of faeries, crouched around the perimeter of the cave. They worked in shifts. Whenever one of the circle grew tired of their mental efforts, that one would be replaced.

"Amergin, my dear," said the Lady Una, using conventional speech rather than her mind, "your defenses are weakening; I can feel it. But you could end the pain now, so very easily. Simply tell us what we want to know." She sat on the ground beneath him, knees tucked up beneath her chin, and smiled sweetly. "What—or who—is this force that opposes us? And how can we overcome it, to claim the power of the Malifex?"

But Amergin had gone. In his mind, he was splashing through the surf, side by side with Eremon and Emer Donn, up onto the shores of Ireland.

✛✛✛

With the setting sun at her back, Charly left the buildings of Hastings behind her and headed out over wilder country. Wheeling over a crumpled landscape of woods and valleys she searched, straining to find a familiar landmark. Normally, she would have been lost, but in this body, she could draw upon senses that would bring a bird safely from Africa to its particular nest site each year, across a thousand miles of sea. Skimming low over the cliffs, something came to her—a particular combination of smell, sight, senses she couldn't even name. Together, they cried out to her: *Here!*

Here was the place she was seeking, Mrs. P.'s special place, the Firehills, where her initiation had taken place. Tumbling from the sky, she landed in the long shadows of the gorse bushes and resumed her human shape.

She walked farther down the hillside, toward the sound of the waves. Her heart was thumping in her chest, but she was torn between fear and excitement. She felt as if she was on the brink of something, something wonderful but scary, like a roller-coaster ride. All she had to do was take the next step, and she would be whisked away into the night, soaring and plummeting.

In an open glade of grass among the dark mounds of gorse, she stopped. The moon had risen now, close to full, and its light cast a track of pale gold across the sea. Charly took a deep breath. *Right*, she thought, *let's see what I can* really *do*.

What she was about to attempt was not strictly forbidden—Wicca had few rules beyond its Rede: *An it harm none, do what thou wilt.* However, there were traditions, ways of doing things. And this was not one of them. Charly had decided to carry out a ceremony called Drawing Down the Moon. In this ceremony, the high priestess of the coven receives the spirit of the Goddess, in effect, *becomes* the Goddess, for the duration of the rite. Since Charly was neither a high priestess nor currently part of a coven, this was unusual to say the least and not without risks. But to rescue Sam she needed power, and this was the fastest way she could think of to obtain it.

The ritual was clear in Charly's mind. She had memorized it long ago, dreaming in her bedroom of the day when she would be a high priestess, wise and graceful, leading her coven in the ways of the Craft. However, since the ritual generally involved several people, she had to frantically edit the words in her head.

Once she had found a formula that would work, she paused, breathing deeply, centering herself. And then, with her arms thrown wide to the moon, she cried out:

I invoke thee and call upon thee, Mighty Mother of us all,
Bringer of all fruitfulness; by seed and root,
By bud and stem, by leaf and flower and fruit,
By life and love do invoke thee
to descend upon the body of this,
Thy servant and priestess.

She stopped, heart pounding, eyes closed. The feeling of standing upon a precipice grew stronger, making her head spin. Taking a deep breath, she continued:

Hail Aradia! From the Amalthean horn
Pour forth thy store of love; I lowly bend
Before thee, I adore thee to the end,
With loving sacrifice thy shrine adore. Um.

She stumbled. The rite called for incense, and she had none. She would have to skip a bit.

Tum-ti-tum, spend thine ancient love,
O Mighty One, descend
To aid me, who without thee am forlorn.

Her head was pounding in time with her heartbeat, and she felt the sweat cool on her skin in the night breeze. She seemed to feel everything more intensely—the movements of the tiny hairs on her upraised arms, small scurryings in the grass, the sharp smell from the sea far below her. She shook her head, trying to find a still point of concentration from which to continue. One last verse, to seal the ritual, to give it its power. Ignoring the waves of sensation sweeping over her, she made the shape of a pentagram in the air above her and called out:

Of the Mother darksome and divine
Mine the scourge, and mine the kiss;
The five-point star of love and bliss
Here I charge you with this sign.

Nothing. And then a silent explosion, a detonation without sound or force, felt only in her mind. Charly staggered and turned around. The hillside behind her was a blaze of golden light. A flame had sprung from every flower of the gorse, a million tiny candles burning clear and bright in the darkness. The sweet smell of coconut was overpowering. She gasped, her face bathed in the yellow radiance as the Firehills poured their tribute into the night sky.

Moving her head to take in the spectacle, Charly found that her vision was blurred. No, not blurred—doubled—as if everything she saw bore an overlay, another layer of meaning drawn across the everyday world like a veil. Nothing was clear or familiar anymore. Turning back, it seemed as if the sea had retreated, for she was now some distance from the shore. A tumbled expanse of rough grass and blazing gorse ran down to a cliff edge, beyond which she could hear the relentless boom and hiss of the waves.

Sensing some presence, she spun around. Behind her was a steep slope. The blazing flowers of the gorse were still there, but another landscape lay over them, older, darker. High up on the skyline, a fire was burning, a plume of sparks streaming away on the steady wind from the sea. A *beacon*, she thought, *the Firehills!*

Charly could hear music, rhythmic drums and the chanting of human voices. The sense of doubled vision made it hard to focus, but she seemed to see a figure moving toward her, picking its way between the dark backs of the gorse bushes.

Charly closed her eyes and took a deep breath, trying to clear her head. When she opened them again, the figure was much closer—a young woman, tall and dark-haired. She was dressed in the clothes of a woodsman or hunter, linen and leather, earth colors, and the light of the moon seemed to cling to her as she walked.

The sensation Charly had before, of heightened senses, was overwhelming now. She heard, felt, saw everything so clearly. A smell of wood smoke from the beacon on the hill, though the wind was blowing away from her. Again, she felt the tiny stirrings of the fine hairs on her arms. She felt the pounding of the distant drums through her feet as much as she heard them.

"Daughter," said a voice.

⊹⊹⊹

"Now then, young Sam," said Wayland, "finish up yer snap and let's set to." The huge smith was bustling around his workshop, gathering together various items. Sam stuffed the last of the bread and cheese in his mouth and stood up, dusting the flour from his hands and clothes.

"I'd make 'ee a sword," continued Wayland, "but it'd be awkerd for 'ee ter swing about, bein' a little 'un. Besides, 'tis the virtue of the iron's the thing, not the size o' the blade. Can't stand any touch o' the stuff, the Faery Folk. No, we'll make 'ee somethin' more suited to yer size."

He brought forth from the recesses of the room a dull, grayish bar of metal, a little shorter than Sam's forearm. "Aye, this'll do," he said, eyeing the metal thoughtfully. "I 'ad a mind ter make summat special wi' this. A day and a night I worked on this"—he waved the bar at Sam— "'eatin' it over charcoal, drawin' it out, foldin' it, 'eatin' again. Takes up some o' the goodness o' the coal, see? Stops it bein' brittle. Aye, this'll do just right."

He took the length of metal over to the great open hearth, where charcoal was glowing gently in the gloom.

"Your job, lad," said Wayland, "is ter tackle to with the bellows." He gestured toward a contraption of wood and leather beside the hearth.

Sam made his way over to where the smith indicated and was hit by a wave of intense heat. Squatting down, he grasped a sweat-polished wooden handle and gave it an experimental tug. As it moved downward, there was a deep *whoosh*, and the charcoal in the hearth glowed yellow. Sparks rushed upward, and the heat almost knocked him over backward.

"Right, lad," said Wayland, "just keep it up."

Sam raised the handle and brought it down once more and again. The charcoal flared, the air shimmered, and Sam settled into the rhythm.

Using a pair of tongs, Wayland placed the length of iron in the fire, at its very heart where the coals glowed almost white. He turned it from time to time, studying it closely, until it too began to glow. When he was satisfied with its color, he took it over to a great anvil mounted on a block of wood and began to hammer. Working along the edges, always in the same direction, Wayland began to draw the blade out, creating a taper from hilt to tip. From time to time, he returned the metal to the fire and waited until the cherry glow returned.

The sweat began to drip from Sam, running down his nose, and he was grateful when Wayland returned the blade to the anvil, so that he could rest his aching arms. The heat and the clangor of the smith's hammer made the air pulsate. And so the hours passed: Wayland intent on his work, his face screwed up in concentration in the ruddy glow of the coals, while Sam alternated between intense activity and periods of boredom. He crouched in the half-light, his hair plastered to his head with sweat as the smith performed his craft.

Occasionally, Wayland would heat the steel to a fierce glow, urging Sam to greater efforts, and then leave it to cool. "Let it rest awhile, lad. And us, too. Reckon we've earned it."

As they rested, Wayland explained to Sam the magic of the bladesmith's trade, how the properties of iron varied according to its composition and the way it was heated, and how the rate at which the iron cooled also affected its quality. An ideal blade, he explained, should be hard enough to keep a sharp edge and yet not so hard that it became brittle and shattered. But it also should be flexible, but not too flexible or it would buckle or lose its edge. And the only way to judge was by experience—by the feel and look of the metal as it heated and cooled, by the way it responded to the hammer.

Then they returned to their labors. Sam toiled away at the bellows handle as Wayland reheated the blade and took it back to the anvil, the sparks leaping as he smote it with his hammer. In the long, hot darkness, the blade took shape—its final outline slender and smoothly tapered, with a metal rod at one end to take the hilt and pommel.

"Time to anneal it," said the smith and placed the metal back in the flames. When it was glowing from end to end, he removed it, wrapped it in pieces of sacking smeared with wet clay, and laid in the embers of the fire. "We'll leave 'un there. Come back in the mornin'."

—✢—

Charly looked up. "Who are you?" she asked. In the years that followed, she rarely spoke of this night, and it was largely because she could never find the words to describe the young woman who stood before her. She was beautiful, more beautiful than anyone Charly had ever seen or heard of. Her skin seemed to glow as if lit from within. Her hair was dark brown and worn in braids, pulled back and gathered behind her head by a bronze pin. She bore a raven on her shoulder. It gazed at Charly along its bristly beak, head on one side, and uttered a low croak. But it was the woman's eyes . . . Charly could never find the words to describe her eyes. They drew her in, the irises of green and hazel spiraling inward to pupils of blackest night. And there, in that darkness, the stars.

"I am Epona," said the voice, and Charly gasped. Epona! A name from her earliest dreams. Although her initiation had come upon her unexpectedly and rather earlier than was usual, Charly had been a good student. She had read her *Book of Shadows*, handed down to her by her mother, and many of the other classical texts on the mysteries of Wicca. Many of these dealt with the various aspects of the Great Goddess, the many names by which the one mother goddess had been known in the cultures of the ages, Greek, Roman, Egyptian, and so on. One of Charly's favorites had always been Epona. She was a horse-goddess of the ancient Celts, a goddess of the Underworld but also of healing and the harvest. She was the only Celtic goddess to have been worshipped in ancient Rome, having been adopted by the Roman cavalry, who discovered her as they fought their way through western Europe. To Charly, brought up on a farm, she had always seemed the ideal goddess, wild and young, a friend to the farmer and to the rider.

"Come," said Epona, "ride with me." She whistled and was answered by a high whinny. A thunder of hoofbeats and a white stallion appeared. It stamped to a halt before them, the breath gusting from its nostrils, blue white clouds in the moonlight. Epona mounted and beckoned for Charly to join her. The raven had flown as the horse approached, drifting silently into the night on soot-black wings. Reaching out for the offered hand, Charly experienced a swirling sensation and found herself on the horse's back, clinging to Epona's waist.

With a mighty kick, the horse took flight, cantering up the slope. As they picked their way through the bushes, the thorns scraping Charly's legs, she saw that they were heading for the fire on the hill's summit. The sound of chanting grew louder. At the foot of the beacon, Epona reined in the horse. It pranced sideways for a moment, reluctant to end its flight. The raven circled them once, then flopped to the ground, hopping out of the reach of stray hooves. Charly looked out over the sea.

"I heard the words of the old ritual, child," said Epona. "You are yet young."

"I–I know. I'm sorry," stuttered Charly. "I was desperate."

"What is it you seek?"

Charly thought for a moment. "Power."

Epona threw back her head and laughed, a wild sound. The horse reared, and Charly clung to the goddess.

"Power? You are a child. What need have you for power?"

"A friend of mine is in trouble. I need to help him," replied Charly sharply.

Epona laughed once more. "Come," she said and with another blur of sensation, Charly found herself on the ground once more, Epona by her side. Looking around, she saw that the horse was gone. Only the raven remained, and with three flaps of its glossy wings, it returned to Epona's shoulder.

The goddess took Charly by the hand and led her to the foot of the beacon. They stood side by side, the great fire roaring above them, the sparks streaming away inland on the wind. Before her the land dropped away, and still Charly had the impression of two worlds, one layered upon the other. Dimly, she could still make out the blazing flowers of the gorse, in the Firehills of her own time. But over them lay another landscape, one much older. As she had noticed before, the sea was much farther away than she remembered. How many centuries, she wondered, would it take for the waves to erode that much land?

Charly saw that Epona was beckoning and moved to follow her. It was difficult to walk. Her doubled vision caused her to stumble as she struggled to keep up with the horse goddess. Cresting the ridge, she paused. Below her, in the lee of the hill, was a hollow. The sound of drums and chanting was coming from a group of huddled figures, their shadows flickering in the light from the beacon. Charly moved closer. As she drew near, the figures were revealed as men in rough clothes of linen and leather, heavy cloaks of animal skin drawn close about them. They bent over something hidden from Charly, some chanting, some beating wide, shallow drums of tanned hide.

"Come closer," said Epona, beckoning. "Do not be afraid."

✛

Sam awoke scratching. He had spent the night on a rough mattress stuffed with straw, in the single room that Wayland shared with his son. Rolling his shirt up, Sam examined the rash that dotted his stomach and chest. He hoped this was from the prickling of the straw, but he suspected that some kind of insect had been involved.

After a breakfast of fresh eggs and more coarse bread, Wayland said, "Now then, lad. Let's see 'ow she's farin'." He set off toward the smithy.

Sam arrived to find the smith lifting the bundle of sackcloth from the cold ashes of the forge and peeling back the layers. The clay had baked solid, and the cloth crackled, shedding clouds of dust as he revealed the contents. Sam reached out and touched the smooth surface. The iron was black and cold now, a dull spike of dark metal marked with the imprint of Wayland's hammer.

"C'mon, boy," said Wayland. He began to build a fire in the center of the forge, heaping charcoal over a pyramid of dry sticks. Sam helped him, and soon they were both covered in black dust, grinning at each other with dazzling eyes and teeth. Wayland struck a spark into a tuft of dry moss, blew on it until a glow bathed his face, and fed it into a gap in the pile of firewood. After more blowing, a tiny flame sprang into life. While Sam watched the fire, the smith worked on the blade with files, grinding and shaping, adding the beginnings of a sharp edge. The metal was soft, easily worked, and quickly took shape under Wayland's expert hands.

The fire blazed for a while, lighting up the dark smithy, then began to settle. With a brittle tinkling, the charcoal collapsed into the embers of the wood and the flames subsided. When the hearth was glowing gently, Wayland added more charcoal and said, "Right, lad. Get on they bellows."

Sam hauled on the bellows handle until the charcoal roared, and Wayland returned the blade to the fire. "Need to 'arden it now," he told Sam. "Get pumpin'."

┿┿┿

Charly gasped, her hand to her mouth. As she drew closer to the circle, she saw that the men were bent over a shallow pit in the earth. Within lay a body, a tall man of middle years, a dusting of gray in his hair. His arms were folded across his chest, and beneath his hands was the pommel of a long sword. He was strewn with the petals of wildflowers, and items of jewelry had been placed about him. Around his neck was a chain of bronze links, and in his hair, clasped to his brow, was a circlet in the form of galloping horses.

"They pray to me now, at the time of death," said Epona, "for the Underworld is mine. You say you seek power. This is power." She gestured at the chanting circle. "The worship of men."

"But that doesn't help me," protested Charly. "Nobody worships me. I'm just a kid."

"No, my child," replied Epona, "for you drew down the moon. The Goddess is within you now. Take up your power."

She led Charly by the hand into the center of the circle. They seemed to pass through the bodies of the men like smoke and found themselves standing by the graveside. The drumming and the relentless drone of voices crowded in on Charly. The two worlds, the ancient and the present day, swirled around her on black wings. She saw images,

107

visions in the streaming sparks from the beacon fire—births, deaths, the galloping of white horses on green fields, harvests of golden wheat, bright swords against the sky. The eye of the moon, high above now, seemed to pierce her, nailing her to the spot. She couldn't breathe. And then, when she thought she would burst, Epona reached out and touched one finger to her forehead.

Suddenly, Charly was at the center of a shaft of light, a pillar of cold radiance that lanced upward into the night sky. She seemed to expand, until she filled the whole world, and the white light spilled out of her, from her eyes, from her mouth. Clenching her fists, Charly drew the radiance into herself, until it formed a white-hot core deep inside. She threw back her head and laughed, high and wild.

"Run with me," said Epona. And Charly ran.

✝✝

Together, they left the circle of shadowy figures and the blazing beacon and ran along the hill's crest. With the speed of horses, they tore across the night, and the cold light of the moon spilled from Charly so that she seemed like a vessel of glass, lit from within. As she ran, her hair streaming behind her, Charly caught glimpses of another figure, half-seen, always on the edge of vision.

"Mother," she called to Epona, "who runs with us?"

"It is my consort, the Horned God. The one you call the Green Man."

Charly turned her head and caught an impression of antlers, a face of leaves and a familiar pair of amber eyes.

"Come," cried Epona and plunged on into the night.

For an eternity, they seemed to run without tiring, along the high ridge. Charly grinned as she ran, exhilarated by the speed, burning within with the power of the Moon Goddess. No longer would she envy Sam his power. This night was hers, had come from her alone. She had her own path to tread now.

After a time that Charly could not measure, the bushes grew thicker and tall trees began to dot the slope. Epona paused, waiting for Charly to catch up. As she drew to a halt, the goddess placed her hands on Charly's shoulders and smiled.

"We are one now, you and I."

"My thanks, Mother," said Charly. Then she added, "I seek a doorway, an entrance to the Underworld."

"There is a gate such as you seek," continued Epona, "It is called the Gate of Water. Follow."

Epona plunged down the slope, leaving the ridge behind and picking her way through the thickening trees. Soon they were in dark woodland, full of strange shadows and movements in the undergrowth.

After a time, Epona led Charly down a steep slope into a narrow valley. Trees arched over from either side, blotting out the stars, but the light of the moon followed them. At the bottom of the valley, splashing and murmuring over rocks, was a tiny stream of cold, clear water. Together, Epona and her daughter followed the flow upward, picking their way slowly through the overhanging branches. At last, they came to a small pool in a bay of rock, where ferns clung to the crevices and water dripped from the moss, a thousand bright droplets.

"The Gate of Water," said Epona, standing aside.

Charly stepped forward. Before her was a blank face of stone, higher than her head, draped with greenery. The source of the stream was somewhere in the rock above her. Water poured down from the leaves of the ferns like strings of glass beads, and its music was all around her.

"Trust," said Epona, "and the gate will open unto you. But take heed, daughter. Those who journey in the Underworld are ever in peril. You have run well on this, your first night of power. But my protection was upon you, and the elder things of the world would not draw near. I will not always be by your side. Fare well, daughter, and blessed be."

"Thank you," replied Charly, feeling awkward. The light that burned within her was fading, and the impression of existing in two worlds at once was drifting away. She gazed at the wall of layered stone. When she looked back, Epona was gone.

Charly stepped forward into the shallow pool at the foot of the waterfall, gasping at the icy bite of the water. She stretched out one hand, meaning to test the weed-draped rock but then decided against it. Trust, Epona had said. Closing her eyes, she strode forward, flinched in expectation, but the anticipated collision never came. Instead, she stumbled, tried to regain her footing, and sprawled headlong into dry dust.

✛

Sam worked until the sweat poured from him, maintaining a steady rhythm that kept the metal glowing red. Just when he thought he was at the end of his endurance,

Wayland took the blade in a pair of tongs and plunged it into a barrel of water. Steam billowed up with a great *whoosh,* and the smith bent close, peering intently at the metal. When he was satisfied, he took it out and returned with it to the forge.

"Right, lad. Now it's 'ard, we needs to temper it." He put the metal back in the coals and let it heat up to a dull glow, cooler than the fiery red that Sam had maintained before, then plunged it once more into the water barrel. He repeated this several times, until at last he seemed happy. Taking the cooled metal from the water, he held it up to his face, squinted along its length with one eye closed, and smiled. "Aye, lad," he said, "that'll do."

"Can I see?" asked Sam, but at that moment, they heard noises outside.

"Stay 'ere," warned Wayland. "I'll go an' see what's amiss."

He stamped out of the forge, and Sam heard muffled voices outside. He listened for a while, trying to gauge the mood of the conversation. As far as he could tell, everything seemed friendly, so he ventured to the doorway.

Wayland was in discussion with a man on a horse, a tall, blond-haired stranger with a haughty expression. Catching sight of Sam, the man said, "And who do we have here, smith?"

"Oh, 'tis just my lad, sir," replied Wayland, "as helps me around the place. Get 'ee back indoors, boy."

Sam turned to go.

"No," said the stranger. "Come here, child." To Wayland, he said, "I've seen your boy, smith. He dresses as you do. This child is different. Come here."

Reluctantly, Sam moved forward.

"What is your name, child?"

Sam looked at Wayland for guidance, but the smith's face remained impassive.

"Sam," he replied.

"Sam," repeated the stranger thoughtfully. "Your name is as strange as your attire, boy. You will come with me. My king will wish to see you." He beckoned for Sam to approach his horse.

"Now, 'ang on," began Wayland, moving to block Sam's path. In an instant, the horseman had drawn his sword with a ringing hiss of steel.

"One more step, smith," he said coldly, "and you will rue the day you forged this blade." He leveled the point at Wayland's chest. "Child, I will not ask again."

Sam stepped toward the horse and was suddenly hauled upward with surprising force. He found himself on the bony spine of the animal, his face pressed against the man's back. As the horse lurched into motion, he flung his arms around the man's waist and hung on for his life. He had one final glimpse of Wayland, standing like a statue outside his forge, as the horse thundered out of the clearing.

⁍⁌

Charly stood in the darkness of the cavern. The magic of the Firehills had faded now, and she felt suddenly very alone. As she waited for her eyes to adjust, she tried to shape a plan in her mind. Sam, she knew, would just blunder off, picking a direction at random. Not her. *Come on,*

Charly, she thought. *Common sense. What would be the sensible way?* She couldn't look for both Sam and Amergin. She had to assume that Sam would make his own way toward the bard. And Amergin would be wherever the Sidhe had their stronghold. So she needed to look for signs of the Sidhe, to try and work out where they were most likely to congregate.

One problem occurred to her right away: Her eyes showed no signs of adjusting to the darkness. She needed light or to be able to see in the dark. And she needed to travel quickly. *Got it!* she thought.

Charly closed her eyes—not that it made much difference—and concentrated on a shape. There was no crop circle here to help her with its residual magic, but she had changed. Part of her, deep down, would always be Epona, the horse goddess.

The change came easily this time. She let out a squeak, too high for the human ear to detect, and its echoes lit up the cavern. She saw—not with her eyes but with her ears—the stalactites and fluted columns that hung from the ceiling, the tumbled boulders and shattered rock of the floor. With a flutter of leathery wings, she darted through a stone arch and headed off along the tunnel, a tiny bat in the echoing darkness.

⊹⊹⊹

Sam was exhausted, his arms like lead. After his efforts on the bellows, there was little energy left in him, and the strain of holding onto the man's waist was unbearable. But the horse continued to canter through the endless forest, and if Sam let go, he would hit the ground at quite a speed. Even in animal form, he was not sure he would survive the fall unscathed. They had galloped along rough paths and dirt tracks for what seemed like an eternity. Once or twice, they had passed through farmsteads, huddles of low buildings where the hens went squawking out of their path and the barking of dogs faded behind them. But the settlements were few and far between. Mostly, they traveled through trees—mighty oaks, ashes, and lindens marching past in an unending procession.

Sam was debating whether or not to attract the man's attention and ask for a rest, when to one side of the trail, the trees began to thin. Above loomed the unmistakable bulk of the Downs. They followed a broad, well-worn track along the foot of the slope, through neatly hedged sheep pasture that gradually gave way to fields of crops. Men were at work with horses or plowing with teams of oxen. Plumes of smoke rose here and there from clusters of buildings, and Sam could hear the distant sound of metal on metal.

The track grew steeper until suddenly, high above them, Sam saw a town. A great fence of sharpened tree trunks circled a high point on the long ridge of the Downs. Within it, Sam could see wooden buildings and pale, shaggy thatch. Smoke rose from here too, a dark smudge across the blue sky.

They reached a broad road up to the town. Outside the towering palisade fence was a deep ditch. The road crossed it on a bridge before plunging between great wooden gates and becoming the main street. Once through the gates, the rider drew his horse to a halt, and Sam slumped gratefully to the ground. He knelt in the dust, massaging his burning arms and groaning.

"Cease your whimpering, boy," snapped the rider, grabbing Sam by the arm and dragging him to his feet. "We go to see my king. Come."

Leading his horse by the reins, he marched up the street, pulling Sam behind him. As he stumbled along, Sam stared around in wonder. The buildings were similar to those he had seen on his journey through the woods but in a far poorer state of repair. Wayland, with none of the conveniences of electricity and running water, still kept his home clean and well maintained and his land in order. Here Sam sensed an air of decay. Children played in puddles of filth in the streets. The thatches of the buildings were gray and sagging. Sam saw rats scurry for cover as a pack of thin, yellowish dogs trotted along the street.

Up ahead, a group of men staggered out of a building and began to brawl in the gutter, cursing and shouting. The rider picked his way carefully around the rolling bodies and continued up the street. At the very crown of the hill was an open square, an area of trampled dirt and scattered household rubbish around the largest building Sam had so far seen. It was low and circular, with a conical roof of thatch rising up to a central hole through which pale blue smoke was drifting. Large wooden doors stood open, but the interior was full of shadow.

As they approached, the rider barked a command, and a young boy ran to take his horse. As the beast was led away, the man said, "You are about to enter the hall of my liege lord, King Haesta. Show respect, speak only when

you are spoken to, and be sure to answer his questions. Or
. . ." He drew his sword a short way from its scabbard, just
far enough for Sam to see the glint of steel. Once more,
the rider grasped his arm and pulled him forward.

It was as if Sam had walked into a vision of hell. In the
center of the great hall, a fire blazed, and the heat it gave
out was stifling. The smoke hung thick in the room,
adding to the gloom. Rough tables were arranged around
the perimeter of the chamber, and men were feasting.
Bones were scattered across the rush-covered floor, and
hunting dogs snarled and brawled over the scraps. As Sam
and the rider entered, the roar of voices lessened until
something approaching silence fell across the gathering.
Darting nervous glances from face to hostile face, Sam was
drawn toward the center of the hall. Beyond the fire, on a
huge throne of wood and wrought iron, sat an equally large
man, his hair and beard blond, and his cheeks flushed red
by the heat and wine.

"My lord," began the rider, "I found this boy at the
smithy. Wayland claims that this is his lad, his assistant.
But he is like no child I have seen before."

The man on the throne leaned forward, one elbow
braced on his knee, and peered at Sam.

"Boy," he rumbled, "account for yourself."

But Sam said nothing. He was staring beyond the
throne, to a dark-haired figure almost lost in the shadows.

"You!" Sam said. "I don't believe it!"

"Forgive me, boy," drawled the voice of the Malifex,
"but should I know you?"

chapter 6

Charly sped on leathery wings through the darkness of the Hollow Hills, swooping between dripping stalactites. The echoes of her voice bounced back to her from a million rock facets and were picked up by her huge, sensitive ears. Her brain converted the echoes into a strangely colorless, grainy image of the world but a precise image. She could judge distances with millimeter precision, flying through gaps barely wider than her outspread wings, darting through a maze of columns and arches.

Soon she saw the first signs of habitation. The floor of the cavern became smoother, worn down by the passage of feet, and the outlines of the archways more regular. Someone—or something—had been at work here, improving on nature, widening and shaping to create underground roadways. And then she began to see a flickering orange light.

Up ahead, a rectangular doorway was outlined by the glow of flames. She swooped close to the ground and reverted to her human shape. Edging forward, she peeped around the doorframe and gasped. Blazing torches in niches on the walls revealed a chamber of wonders. Along one side of the room was a Viking longboat, perfectly preserved, its dragon-headed prow casting a sinister shadow across the floor. Along the facing wall was a row of suits of armor, some plain and functional, others ornate and highly decorated. Swords and shields of all sizes and designs hung from the columns that supported the roof. In the center of the chamber, in pride of place, stood a huge cannon and its cannonballs, neatly stacked. Charly realized that this collection represented a history of warfare spanning centuries, but all the items looked as if they had been made only yesterday.

She moved on, past chain-mail shirts and racks of spears, to a doorway on the opposite side of the room. Here more torchlight glinted from golden plates and goblets, from open chests of jeweled crowns and necklaces. Resisting the urge to stop and rummage through the chests, Charly made her way through the treasure chamber and out by another door. This time, she found herself in a broad hallway with a high, vaulted ceiling. Flaming torches were arranged along the walls at regular intervals, fading away into the far distance. Since there was enough light for her to see, Charly decided to stay in human form. But she felt increasingly nervous. The chambers she had passed through contained an unimaginable fortune— surely the Sidhe would not leave them unguarded? After a moment's thought, she closed her eyes. When she opened them again, she was clad from head to foot in black—a flowing black satin skirt over black leggings and leather motorbike boots, a black leather jacket over a black T-shirt. Even her auburn hair was now a glossy shade of midnight. With a satisfied smile, she strode off along the chamber.

╋╋╋

Amergin sprawled in the dust in the center of the room. The circle of Sidhe who had kept him suspended in the air were gone, their work done. He moaned and tried to push himself up from the floor, but the pain in his shoulder joints was too intense, and he slumped back, exhausted.

So, thought Finnvarr to the Lady Una, *it was the boy after all. We have made a grave error.*

I don't understand, my lord, replied Una. *How did the spirit of Attis come to reside in this . . . this child?*

That, I think, is a tale our friend here, he prodded Amergin in the chest with the toe of his boot, *has yet to tell us. For now, it is enough to know that the power of the Green Man survives, and it is all that stands between us and our goal. Destroy the spirit of the Green One, and the power of the Malifex will be ours.*

So we seek the boy?

Perhaps. And perhaps not. Lord Finnvarr paused for a moment, lost in thought. *The boy is involved somehow, but he is not Attis. No, the power of the Green Man is dispersed, like that of the Malifex. It is strong in the boy, but it is not rooted in him. It will manifest soon, though, for a moment.*

At the festival?

Indeed. I think we should pay a visit to the castle and await the coming of the May King.

And what of him? Lady Una nodded at the motionless

form of Amergin, sprawled in the dirt before them.

Leave him, said Finnvarr. *Seal the door. And when all this is over, there are stories I would like to hear from our friend the Milesian.*

┼┼┼

Sam stared in astonishment at the Malifex. "Er, sorry," he stammered, "you, um, reminded me of someone."

The Malifex frowned back at him from behind the throne. Sam felt a familiar prickling in his mind.

Boy, said a voice in his head, *there is something strange about you. I'm sure we have never met and yet, there is a hint of my brother about you. . . .*

The voice receded, and the Malifex bent close to the ear of the king on his throne, whispering.

After a moment, King Haesta leaned forward and said, "Boy, it seems my counselor has not only never seen you before, he has never seen your like. And Counselor Morfax has traveled far. What are you, boy?"

"Just a boy, sir," replied Sam, casting his eyes to the ground. "I work for Wayland, the smith, sort of an apprentice."

The lord frowned and turned again to his counselor. There was another whispered conversation.

"Child," continued Haesta, returning his gaze to where Sam stood, head bowed, "we have seen Wayland's lad, and you are not he. Nor do we know this word, *apprentice*. So it seems you lie to us. Perhaps you are a foreign spy or worse—some fell creature of magic. It will be amusing to find out. Bind him."

120

Sam felt his arms seized from behind and began to struggle. A coarse rope was looped around his wrists, biting into the flesh. He felt a wave of panic sweep over him and almost instinctively shifted shape. The two men who were attempting to bind his wrists found themselves wrestling with a large and angry wolf. With cries of fear, they released him and fell back. Sam stood in the center of the room, ears flat against his skull, the soft gray fur on his spine bristling. A low growl came from his throat. Otherwise, the room was silent. No one moved.

And then Sam felt a familiar presence in his mind. *I thought as much,* said the Malifex. *You stink of my brother. I did not know he had taken to training pets. Well, let us see how well he has taught you.*

Without moving or otherwise betraying his powers, the Malifex began to assault Sam's mind. Time seemed to stand still, the faces of Haesta and his guards frozen in expressions of amazement. Waves of malice beat against Sam, forcing him backward, stiff-legged, step-by-step. His lips were pulled back from his teeth and the long, low growl seemed loud in the unnatural silence. He tried to throw up some sort of shield, a barrier in his mind against the evil radiance coming from the still form of the Malifex. But as he concentrated, his shape slipped, and he was Sam once more. As he slumped to the floor, a wave of angry noise washed over him as time began to flow once more. Men shouted and cursed, scrambling backward in fear. King Haesta called for his guards, and the Malifex, standing quietly behind the throne, merely smiled.

Not good enough, boy, came the voice in Sam's head.

121

Still, perhaps one day—

And then rough arms grabbed him from behind. A voice cried, "Take him outside!" and he felt himself dragged backward, heels bouncing on the rough earth floor, toward the door.

News of the excitement had spread around the town. A crowd began to gather. From houses and taverns, running figures converged on the central square. Sam was lifted up onto the shoulders of several of the king's guards and found himself bouncing across the heads of the crowd, sky above him, noise and the stink of unwashed bodies beneath his back.

Then the crowd parted, and Sam was thrown to the ground. He rolled, the air knocked from his lungs, and sprawled to a halt in the dust. Gasping for breath, he pushed himself up and looked around. Dusk was falling, and in the soft twilight, he saw that he was in the wide square of trampled earth at the heart of the town. Not far away, he could see the low circular building that served as the king's feasting hall, the plume of smoke rising from its thatch tinged pink by the light of the setting sun. The crowd had pulled back, whispering and muttering, forming a rough circle around him. Children clung to their parents' legs, excited and scared by the rumors of magic. As Sam peered at them, they gasped and hid in their mothers' skirts.

Slowly, with great effort, Sam got to his feet and stood swaying in the middle of the circle of faces. The efforts of the day were beginning to catch up with him, and he felt weak and dizzy. To one side, the crowd parted and Haesta strode into the square, with the Malifex, as always, at his shoulder. The muttering of the crowd ceased.

With his hands on his hips, the king said, "It is clear that you are some sort of wizard or evil spirit. Counselor Morfax, however, seems to believe that you can be killed, and so we will attempt it. Now, what, I wonder, is the best way to destroy you?" He turned to the Malifex, and the two of them began a whispered conversation.

Sam became aware of a commotion in the crowd, where the main street of the town entered the square. Gradually the stirring spread, and the crowd began to part. Through the gap rode Wayland on what appeared to be a cart horse. He reined the horse to a standstill. The crowd fell silent. King Haesta broke off his conversation and looked up.

"Smith, what is the meaning of this?" he demanded.

"I've come for the boy," replied Wayland, steadily.

╾╂╈╂╾

Amergin swam back up to consciousness like a man surfacing from deep water. Suddenly, he found himself gasping in the cool air of the cave, the blood roaring in his ears. For a moment, he thought he was on the shore of Ireland, thrown onto the sands of a new land by the stormy sea, but the darkness and the *drip, drip* of water said otherwise. Then he remembered. He had been hanging in the center of a cave in a world of agony, his mind fleeing through visions of the past, with the voices in his head, tormenting, questioning, demanding. Finally, he recalled with horror, his defenses had fallen, and the probing mind had picked from his exhausted brain one choice thought:

123

an image of Sam, his eyes the color of amber, soft tendrils of foliage spilling from the corners of his mouth.

Slowly, the realization dawned on him that he was not alone. Without moving, he cast out his mind to Finnvarr and Una, their thoughts almost audible.

At the festival? he picked up from Una, and from Finnvarr, . . . *await the coming of the May King.*

So that was it. They would attack the festival at the castle, break the power of the Green Man at the moment when he manifested as the May King. With the spirit of the Green Man broken, dispersed, his power—and that of the Malifex—would be taken by the Sidhe. Control of the cycles of nature, birth and death, the turning seasons, would fall to the Hosts of the Air, whose hatred of humankind spanned millennia.

Amergin sensed that the faeries were leaving and risked opening one eye. As they left the chamber, the Lady Una turned and made a gesture with one hand. A web-work of pale lavender energy sprang into being across the doorway, sealing Amergin inside. The wizard sighed and pressed his cheek against the cold rock of the floor.

✢

Megan and Mrs. P. sat in the old lady's attic room, the light of the moon slanting in through the high window in the end wall. The room was crammed with old furniture, richly polished desks and bookcases. There was nothing of the tackiness of the downstairs rooms here. Everything had an air of age and quality. Like Megan's study back in Dorset, every available surface was laden with books and

124

artifacts—scientific instruments in gleaming brass, lumps of rock encrusted with fossils, incense burners, candles in elaborate holders. At one end of the room, in the one area relatively free from clutter, was a small altar, with a silver chalice, a wand of rowan wood, a small, exquisite athame—a black-handled knife—and a pentagram.

Megan sat with her legs tucked up beneath her, seeming calm and still. But Mrs. P. could sense otherwise. She could read an aura better than Megan, having had many more years in which to practice. And Megan's aura was thick with worry, violent colors swirling in constant agitation.

"My dear," she said, looking up from her work, "do try to calm down. You're playing absolute havoc with the vibrations."

"Sorry," replied Megan distractedly. But try as she might she could not drag her thoughts from their downward spiral. It seemed as if her life were falling apart. First, Amergin taken from her, who knew where. Then Sam . . . what on earth was she going to tell his parents? And now her baby, her Charly, newly initiated into the Craft and out in the dark hills, alone. She had gone to Charly's room to make peace and found her gone, the drapes flapping in the open window. She chewed absently at a fingernail and stared blindly into the moonlit dark.

Mrs. P. bent once more to the sphere of clear crystal on the desk before her, trying to shut out the background hiss of Megan's thoughts. Her heart ached for her friend. Over the years, she had initiated many young girls into the Craft of the Wise, all of them as dear to her as daughters, all of them—when the time came—making that painful break.

The heartache brought wisdom, in time, but all the wisdom in the world could not comfort a mother newly separated from her daughter. Still, in a way, she was glad that her friend was distracted. Her own aura, at that precise moment, did not bear close scrutiny.

Time passed, and the silver minute hand of moonlight swept slowly across the carpet. Eventually, Megan could stand it no more. "Well?" she demanded, her voice loud in the silence. "Does it tell you anything? Is she all right?"

"She is well," replied Mrs. P. "Far from here—I do not know where—but well."

"And Amergin?"

"He . . . is lost."

Megan gasped, a look of sudden horror on her face.

"No, my dear, not dead, but . . . lost to us. He wanders in his mind, I think, in places I cannot follow. But he lives. Sam, I cannot see, but I feel it in my bones that he is well. Some higher power, I sense, protects him."

Megan slumped back in her chair, eyes shut against tears of relief.

"There is more," continued the old lady. "The Sidhe are plotting, planning some evil. It involves the festival tomorrow. I think we should send out word among the Wise. I feel we will be needed."

"Right!" Megan unfolded from the chair in one fluid motion. "I'll get on the phone, start letting people know." Relieved to find an outlet for her tension, she bustled out of the room.

Mrs. P. watched her go with a mixture of affection and pride. Megan had always been one of her favorites. She sat quietly, gazing out of the window at the dance of moon-light on the sea, remembering Megan's initiation. But slowly, inevitably, her thoughts returned to what she had seen in the crystal ball. So many rituals down through the years, not only initiation and the marriage rite—the Handfasting—but also that other, more somber ritual, the Rite for the Dead. You would think that, as one who had presided for so long over the turning of the Wheel of Life, her own death would come as no surprise. *Oh, well,* she sighed, *so much for wisdom.* But one thing age had taught her was the futility of brooding. She took a deep breath and got to her feet. If she was to have one last adventure, then there were preparations to make.

╋╋╋

Charly strode along the hallway, the soft padding of her boots loud in the silence. The twin rows of burning torches in their niches stretched away into the distance, almost converging at the vanishing point. They seemed to burn without smoke and with no sign that anyone attended to them. Their steady light barely illuminated the arches of the ceiling, far above. The air of the cham-ber, shielded from whatever season or weather prevailed in the world outside, was mild, and Charly began to feel uncomfortable in her leather jacket and boots. She had been walking for some time, and still the long hallway showed no signs of coming to an end. She wondered if she was in fact moving at all. The twin rows of torches and towering pillars marched by without any feature to mark her progress. She glanced behind, half expecting to see the exit from the treasure chamber. Instead, there were only the torches stretching away behind, but they seemed to stop a few hundred meters back. As she watched, the farthest pair of torches went out. And then the next. A wave of darkness was moving toward her along the hall, snuffing out the flames two by two.

Charly turned back and began to walk more quickly. *Perhaps it's the wind,* she thought, knowing as she did so that the air was completely still. Now she could hear a strange sound, a kind of hissing and murmuring, as though an unseen host of people was conversing in soft voices. She glanced back once more and saw that the darkness was drawing closer, faster than she could walk. She broke into a jog, wondering how long she could keep it up. Then, to her horror, she saw that up ahead the torches came to an end as they had behind, in a pool of darkness. She looked back over her shoulder and screamed. Like a black tidal wave, a sweeping shadow was bearing down upon her. And within it were creatures from her worst nightmares. Forgotten beasts from the elder days—driven underground along with the Sidhe, their masters—poured down the hall. The *cu sith,* huge black dogs with eyes of flame, loped toward Charly. Behind them came bugganes, shape-shifting from goblin to ram to giant bull. Swooping and flapping through the air, carrying the darkness to the high vaulted ceiling, were banshees, beautiful faery women with flowing black hair and fangs, who drank human blood. Farther back, lost in the black tide, were shapes Charly could not make out, terrible shapes. She screamed once more and broke into a run. Although there was darkness before her, she fled in terror from the horror behind her, from night into night.

But as she ran, she made out a faint rectangle in the wall ahead, picked out in a flicker of firelight. The end of the torches ahead marked only the end of the long hallway, and Charly was within reach of a doorway.

In blind panic, she ran down the last stretch, expecting with every pulse of her laboring heart to feel the breath of the black dogs on her neck. The boots she had created for herself rubbed against her heels and sweat was pouring down her spine within the leather jacket, but still she pushed herself onward. The noise—the immense, whispering wall of sound—was so close now it seemed to swirl around her as the rectangle of firelight grew, slowly, so painfully slowly. A red haze began to grow around the edges of Charly's vision, and each breath burned in her chest like flame.

And then the doorway was before her, the comforting flicker of firelight playing on its stone frame. She lunged toward the opening, boots skidding on the dusty floor, and flailed to a halt on the threshold. The room before her fell silent as the Host of the Sidhe paused from their feasting and looked up at her.

✛

"Smith," said King Haesta, "this is not your boy. In fact, it is not even a boy. It is a dwarf wizard of some sort. In your place, I would not wish to claim allegiance with a wizard sentenced to death."

"As yer like," replied Wayland. "Still, I've come for the

boy, an' I ain't leavin' without 'im."

"In that case—" Haesta sighed. "You will die with him. Guards."

Soldiers with iron spears and swords stepped forward. Wayland slid from the back of his horse and dropped to the ground. It seemed to Sam as though the ground shook as his feet hit the earth of the square. From a sling on his back, the smith drew a hammer, a lump of blue gray iron the size of his two fists, mounted on the end of a long wooden handle. He dropped the hammerhead to the ground between his feet and rested his hands on the handle's upper end.

"Sam, me lad," said the smith, "we better be takin' us leave o' these folk. Down the high street, if yer please."

Sam made to move, and the guards started forward to stop him. With incredible speed, the smith's hammer lashed out, and two of the guards dropped to the ground, moaning.

"Go on, lad!" exclaimed Wayland. "Don't stand sowin' gape seed. Shift it!" Sam closed his mouth and began to push through the crowd, heading for the long main street. No one seemed inclined to stop him. However, looking back he saw that Wayland was surrounded by a growing number of the king's guards. Fearing for his friend, he paused. The smith's hammer was whirling around his head, almost too fast for Sam to follow. The hum it made as it cut through the air was punctuated by the crack of bone. More guards poured into the square, but as he fought, Wayland seemed to grow. He was a good head taller than the largest of his opponents now, and a light seemed to be flowing out of his skin. As Sam watched, the smith became taller still and broader. Throwing back his head, he bellowed with laughter as the huge hammer hummed and sang. Sam decided it was safe to leave the smith to his work and slipped through the back of the crowd into the street beyond. Despite his exhaustion, he managed to jog down the slope toward the town gate. Soon he heard footsteps behind him and turned. To his relief, it was the smith, grinning fiercely, covered with scratches and cuts but otherwise unscathed.

"Right then, young Sam," panted the smith, "we needs get you back on yer quest to 'elp yer friend." Outside the gate, he gestured to the right and led Sam around the curve of the hill, following the crest of one of the great defensive ditches that encircled the town. A quarter of the way around the town's perimeter, Wayland pointed to a slight rise, a smaller version of the hilltop on which the town stood. Here a beacon fire was burning, throwing sparks up into the deepening twilight.

"That's where we're 'eaded," explained the smith. Sam looked puzzled but was content to follow. They crossed the ditch on a narrow wooden bridge and headed up the gentle slope onto the very crest of the Downs. Gazing out over the landscape below, the strangeness of his situation hit Sam like a hammer blow. Where he would have expected the orange map work of streetlights was . . . nothing. A rolling blanket of blue gray woodland stretched out under the soft evening air to the dying stain of the sun on the far horizon. What was he doing here, so far from home? He heard a grunt from Wayland and turned.

Something moved across the darkened turf of the hilltop toward them, a blur of deeper darkness that resolved itself into the figure of the Malifex. The smith pulled his hammer from its sling once more.

"Boy," began the Malifex, standing before them, hands on hips, "I don't know who—or what—you are, but you have powerful friends. Well met, Volund." He nodded to the smith, who stared calmly back.

"Your friend here," the Malifex continued to Sam, "is the son of Wate, the sea giant. Almost a god. But not quite, eh?"

Wayland shrugged.

"But you, boy, you are a puzzle. My brother's stench is all over you, but he is not one for meddling in human affairs. Strange. . . . There is clearly a tale to be told here. Sadly, though, I fear I will have to kill you and leave it untold."

He drew back one hand, fingers clawed.

"Sam!" shouted the smith. "Into the fire!"

"What?" Sam looked horrified.

"The Gate of Fire! Quick!"

The Malifex unleashed a bolt of energy, violet lightning crackling through the air. Quick as thought, the smith's hammer flew into its path, deflecting it harmlessly to the side.

"You're a Walker Between Worlds, lad," called Wayland. "Just think of where you want ter go and trust."

Sam turned from the smith to the beacon fire, a blazing pyre of logs on the hill's summit, spitting sparks into the sky. His mouth went dry. The Malifex had turned his attention to Wayland now. The two of them were locked in battle, the smith huge once more and full of glee, glowing with his own power. The Malifex hurled bolt after bolt of malice, but Wayland parried with his hammer, occasionally lashing out to strike the Malifex with a force that shook the hill.

Sam looked back at his friend, and as he did, Wayland turned briefly.

"'Ere," he shouted, "don't forget this!" He threw a cloth-bound bundle to Sam. "Fare well, lad. And give they Farisees one from me!" With that he returned to his battle.

Sam gazed once more into the heart of the fire, where the ragged remnants of branches glowed almost white. Then he closed his eyes and walked toward the blaze. As the heat grew, he heard the Malifex shout, "One day, boy! This is not over!"

chapter 7

The Host of the Sidhe stared at Charly for a moment and then returned to their feasting. Charly stood panting, holding onto the door frame for support. The memory of horror made her spin around, but the long hallway behind her was empty, the torches flickering once more in their niches.

She closed her eyes for a moment, trying to slow her heartbeat. Her mouth was filled with thick, acid saliva, and her lungs ached. Swallowing with a grimace, she adjusted her hair and took a deep breath. Then, with as much innocence as she could muster, she strolled into the feasting hall.

Arrayed in their finery, the Hosts of the Air ate and drank to the sweet music of pipes and fiddles. At the head of the great table, Lord Finnvarr and Lady Una sat side by side, smiling indulgently at their subjects. They seemed oblivious to Charly, who kept close to the wall, circling around the tables, a look of studied innocence on her face. For a moment, however, she glanced to the top table and her eyes met with those of the Lady Una. But only for a moment. The Faery Queen broke the contact and turned her attention to some story being told by a courtier.

Charly tried to keep her face neutral, but the familiar feeling of hatred had welled up when she had looked into Una's eyes. She continued around the perimeter of the room, staying in the shadows. Suddenly, a hand grabbed her arm and her heart nearly stopped.

"Come!" said a rich, musical voice. "Sit here. The evening is yet young!"

Charly found herself staring into the face of a tall young man with flowing black hair and lavender eyes. "Um," she mumbled, trying to think of an excuse as she found herself propelled toward a chair. Feeling suddenly more shy than scared, she sat down. The young man began to load her plate with delicacies—slices of meat and strange fruit, rich cheeses, and soft white bread. Charly tried the bread, thinking that it, at least, ought to be safe, and found it was delicious. She began to try the other items on her plate and discovered that they were all exquisite. She washed the food down with a pale, golden liquid from a silver goblet. It tasted a little like honey, but refreshing rather than sickly, like cold spring water. The sweet voices of the faery host swirled around her as she ate, and the warmth from the huge fire burning in the hearth along one wall soaked into her bones, relaxing her aching muscles.

At the head of the table, a silent exchange took place between Lord Finnvarr and the Lady Una.

So our pets have brought us a gift—the mortal girl, thought the Lord of Sidhe. *We will have good sport with her. Perhaps as a finale to the feast.*

No, my lord, replied Lady Una. *Spare her, I beg you!*

Finnvarr raised one eyebrow. *You feel pity for*

this . . . mortal?

No, my lord. Unfinished business lies between us.

Finnvarr threw back his head and roared with laughter. *Ah, my queen! Take her then, my gift to you. But be swift. We must make ready for war.*

✛✛

Before long, Charly began to feel a little dizzy. The sounds of merrymaking seemed to grow distant, and she had trouble keeping her eyes open. She let her head slump down onto her chest and stared at her plate. It was littered with the remains of her meal—puddles of congealed sauce, unidentifiable bones and scraps of meat, cheese rind, shining globules of fat. Charly felt ill. Dreading the thought of being sick at the table, she willed herself to rise, but the heat and the incessant music wrapped around her brain. She felt removed, distant from her own body. With an effort, she turned her head and looked up the length of the long table. She found the Lady Una staring right back at her. The smirking face of the faery sent a cold surge of fury through Charly, clearing her head. With an effort of will, she mumbled "'Scuse me" to the man with the lavender eyes and got to her feet. Unsteadily, she made her way around the room and through a door into the fresh air of the corridor beyond.

✛✛

The day of the festival dawned cold and gray, a thin overcast moving in off the sea, threatening rain. Megan dragged herself from her bed with a feeling of dread. Today she would have to set up her stall in the castle grounds and go about her business, not knowing if Charly, Amergin, and Sam were alive or dead. And if Mrs. P. was right, something terrible would happen before the festival was over.

She set off early, leaving Mrs. P. to bustle around the Aphrodite, cooking breakfasts and telephoning her friends, warning them of the day's coming threat. Her car labored up the steep streets of the Old Town, onto the top of West Hill. There Megan was relieved to find a parking space close to the castle entrance. Taking a fold-up table from the trunk, she walked up the long entrance track, waved her stallholder's pass at the woman in the ticket office, and made her way out into the ruins of the castle.

The castle, built by William the Conqueror to commemorate his victory over the English in 1066, was destroyed by King John just one hundred and fifty years later. Time and the elements had continued his work, until all that remained were a few tumbledown walls and the roofless shells of buildings surrounding a bowl of grass, perched on the lip of the cliffs.

A few people were already at work, setting up their stalls or ferrying food and drink to the big white tents along one wall. Megan exchanged greetings with a few of the other stallholders, regulars like herself, and began to set up her table. Several trips later, the stall was complete, the pottery arranged neatly on a brightly colored tablecloth. Megan wandered over to the seaward side of the castle, where a low and ragged wall separated the grassy arena from the steep cliff face. From there, she could look out over the town. Far below, a long car park on the seafront had been taken over by motorbikes, hundreds of them in gleaming rows. The massed roar of their engines drifted up to the castle on the damp salt wind. Beyond the bikes, the flat gray expanse of the sea merged seamlessly with the sky. Tracking across the rows of bikes, Megan's eyes found a knot of color and movement: the beginnings of the festival. Down on the promenade, out beyond the car park, the procession was forming. Megan could just make out the straggling line of Jack's followers, dancing figures in green and black and, at the center of the procession, the towering shape of Jack himself—the Green Man.

Megan smiled a small, tired smile. Through the cold and damp of spring, the May King was coming, bringing in the summer. There was always hope.

┽┽

Charly paused for a moment. The fresh air, after the heat and noise of the banqueting hall, made her head spin, and she had to press her hands against the wall to stop herself from falling. She leaned her forehead against the cool rock, waiting for the feeling of dizziness to pass. When she felt more in control of herself, she wiped the cold sweat from her face and set off along the corridor.

The stronghold of the Sidhe was a maze of tunnels and passageways, with countless rooms opening off left and right. She passed kitchens and mess halls, dormitories and storerooms, as she wandered aimlessly in the half-light. After some time, with no clear idea of where she was going, she stopped. *OK, lady,* she thought, *this is no good. I could blunder around down here for hours. Time to flex the old thinking muscle.* Placing one hand on the stone of the passage wall, she tried to send her mind into the rock, seeking some hint of Amergin. At first, her consciousness stopped dead at her fingertips. She could feel only the gritty texture against her skin, the sheen of moisture. The more she concentrated, the more clearly she could feel each tiny grain of rock like a pebble against the spiraling patterns of her fingertips. And suddenly, as if a window had opened in her mind, she felt beyond her fingers, into the stone itself. Pushing outward, her mind expanded into the huge mineral bulk of the hillside.

Everywhere, Charly sensed the taste of the Sidhe, the faint prickling feeling of wrong she felt when in their presence. Furrowing her brow, she brought more and more of the three-dimensional landscape of stone into her mind's eye, until it hung in space before her. Then she saw it: a tiny pool of *otherness,* a place where the stink of the Sidhe was replaced by something else, something familiar, comforting. Amergin. Smiling, Charly set off in search of the wizard.

✛

The feast was over. Lord Finnvarr sent his followers off to make their final preparations, stirring promises of glory and power ringing in their heads. In the confusion, Lady Una slipped from his side, making her way around the room and out through a side door. With a look of mischief on her delicate features, she stepped lightly along the corridor.

The last of the Host dispersed, and silence fell in the great banqueting hall. The fire in the broad hearth was dying down now, the last few logs glowing in the gloom.

Suddenly, a figure burst from the heart of the fire, appearing out of the heat shimmer with a gasp. Sprawling onto the floor, Sam rolled, one hand still clutching the package Wayland had thrown to him, and came up hard against a table leg. He lay still for a few moments, colored lights wheeling behind his eyes and smoke rising from the soles of his shoes. Scrambling to his feet, he surveyed the long table, which was littered with the remains of the faery banquet.

His stomach wrenched with hunger, and he grabbed a handful of fruit from a bowl, stuffing sweet berries into his mouth. Next, he ripped off a hunk of white bread and chewed greedily on it as he poured a gobletful of golden liquid from a silver pitcher. Perhaps it was the intense hunger, but the food was the best he had ever tasted. He gulped at the golden drink and then surveyed the table. Making his way along its length, he picked and nibbled at the leftovers, a piece of creamy white cheese here, a slice of meat there. Finally, his hunger satisfied, he slumped into a chair and swung his feet up onto the table.

Then he remembered the package. Opening the wrappings, he saw the knife. Wayland had polished the blade of the athame to a soft sheen, bringing out a delicate spiraling pattern, like repeated snowflakes, deep within the metal. A black wooden handle was bound in place by bands of bronze and topped off with a disk of iron. Looking more closely, Sam could make out something engraved on the circle of metal. He smiled. It was a human face surrounded by leaves, tendrils of foliage emerging from its mouth and nose. Standing up, Sam flipped the knife into the air and caught it, unfortunately by the blade rather than the handle. With a yelp, he dropped it and looked at his hand, but it was unmarked. From a silver salver he chose an apple, huge and artificially red, and tested the athame against its skin. The knife slid through as if through water. Sam peered at the blade, tested it with his thumb: blunt. He glanced back at the two halves of the apple, lying on the table. They seemed to have shrunk and to have aged dramatically. Brown spots marked the wrinkled skin. *That's odd*, he thought. It was as if the apple had been enchanted, and the magic had vanished at the touch of iron. Sam felt queasy as he wondered exactly what he had just been eating. He tucked the athame into his belt. Looking around the room, he spotted a door off in the shadows and made his way toward it.

✛

Amergin sat with his head bowed, staring into a darkness that was as much in his mind as in the room around him. He had been foolish. He had thought, when Sam defeated the Malifex, that his long quest was over, his task completed, and he had relaxed. With his head full of television and flying machines, he had turned his back on the old ways—on his heritage—and fallen into folly. And this was the result, trapped like a fly by the webs of his ancient enemy. What would his old mentor, Merlin, say if he could see him now?

Actually, came a voice in his mind, *not a lot, under the circumstances.*

Amergin spun around and caught a faint glimpse of movement, but when he looked more closely, there was

141

nothing there. He sighed, fearing that, at the bitter end, his mind was failing him.

What with all the business about that witch Nimue, continued the voice, *you know, imprisoning me all these years, I'm not really in a position to comment about folly.*

"Merlin?" Amergin called into the dead air. He thought he heard a chuckle.

I suppose what I'm saying, said the voice, *is that we all make mistakes, let our guard down. With me, it was the ladies. With you it was—What is Buffy? Never mind.*

Amergin was on his feet now, eyes darting around the room. In the faint light from the webwork of energy across the doorway, he thought he could see movement, as if someone was constantly stepping out of the edge of his field of vision. But whenever he turned to look, there was nobody there.

The important thing is to get over it. Move on. The voice seemed to draw closer. *My friend, you once called yourself Wisdom. Use your head, wise man. The story*—the voice was so close now—*never ends. The circle, remember? Always turning. Down through all the years, evil will rise and fall, and always the wise and the brave will stand forth to oppose it. Your task is not over, no more than mine. The power that was in the Malifex cannot be destroyed, merely weakened for a time. And you and I, old friend, we will fight it whatever form it takes.*

The voice seemed to recede. "Merlin!" cried Amergin. "I . . ."

Go, Bard of the Milesians. Your young Arthur needs you.

And the voice was gone.

Amergin sat for a moment, lost in thought, then scrambled painfully to his feet. Merlin was right. His labors were not yet over. He took a deep breath, shaking off the despair that had sapped his will. Reaching inside, he found a hidden core of strength that the Sidhe had not broken. With a glint of anger in his eye, he turned and hurled a bolt of energy at the doorway. It shattered the web of the Sidhe into a million fragments. Writhing worms of purple energy glowed and sparked on the ground for a moment and then were gone.

✛

Charly moved quickly along a dark passageway that angled down into the earth. She had left behind the store-rooms and kitchens, the barracks and armories, and entered an area that seemed almost abandoned. She had seen no one since leaving the banqueting hall, but here the dust and the infrequent torches suggested that the Sidhe seldom ventured this way.

Suddenly, she heard footsteps behind her and spun around. "You!" she exclaimed. It was Sam. She took a few steps toward him, grinning with relief, before she remembered herself. Planting her hands on her hips, she snapped, "You left me. You absolute, steaming, twenty-four carat *boy!*" She spat the last word as if it was the worse insult she could find.

Sam shrugged his shoulders and gave her an embarrassed grin. "Sorry?" he tried.

"Sorry? Is that the best you can do?" she exploded. "You go tearing off into the hills, without so much as—"

"Well, I'm here now," interrupted Sam. "Let's go and find Amergin, shall we?"

With that he pushed past her and headed off down the passage. Charly stood with her mouth working for a moment, then set off after him. "Don't you even want to know if I'm OK?" she demanded as she caught up.

"You look fine to me," replied Sam, not looking round. "Come on—this way."

Just then, Charly heard footsteps once more, running this time. "Watch out," she hissed to Sam, "someone's coming."

They hurried around a corner and found themselves in a chamber where four passageways converged. Sam stepped into the darkness of one of the side passages and dragged Charly after him, motioning for her to be quiet. From the shadows, they saw a figure stumble to a halt in the torchlight, looking around in confusion. As he turned toward them, Charly saw it was Sam. With a cry, she stepped out into the chamber.

"Charly!" said the second Sam. "Look, about leaving you . . . "

"Don't listen to him," said the first Sam, stepping out of the shadows. "It's some trick of the Sidhe. Look, he's got some sort of knife."

And Charly saw that indeed the newly arrived Sam was holding a long dagger limply by his side. "Charly?" he said. "What's—"

"Now hang on a minute," demanded Charly, "you can't both be the real Sam. So we need to sort you out. Any suggestions? You . . . " She pointed to the second Sam.

"Um, I dunno . . . how about—"

"A test," butted in the first Sam. "Ask us some questions, something that only I would know, something that the Sidhe could never have found out."

Charly was edging toward the first Sam as he spoke, casting worried glances from face to familiar face.

"How about, instead—" and with surprising speed she pivoted on one foot and kicked the first Sam firmly in the stomach. "Kill it!" she screamed.

The newly arrived Sam stood blankly for a moment, looking from Charly to his double to the knife in his hand. Then he grunted, "Oh, right!" and took a couple of steps forward.

The Lady Una straightened up, rubbing her stomach, eyes fixed on Sam's athame. Edging toward the mouth of the nearest tunnel, she hissed to Charly, "You will pay for this, mortal. You and all your kind." And then, as Sam lunged toward her with his blade, she cast a fold of her black lace skirt before his face and vanished in a vortex of air.

"Oh, well done, Zorro," said Charly as the dust settled. "That showed her."

Sam opened his mouth to speak, then paused.

"How did I know which one was you?" asked Charly.

"Er, yeah."

She smiled, shaking her head, "Sam, you stood there with your mouth open, grunting 'dunno,' holding that knife as if somebody had handed you a wet fish, and you ask me how I knew?" She chuckled. "Come on, let's find Amergin."

Sam closed his mouth, then ran to catch up with Charly as she strode off along the tunnel.

"Hey," he shouted, "that's not fair! I came to rescue you! I didn't have to, you know!"

"Yeah, yeah, yeah," breathed Charly, still smiling.

╬

Jack-in-the-Green bobbed and twirled through the streets of the town, accompanied by his bogeys and followers and by a growing crowd of tourists. The sound of the accordion and a jingle of bells, the stamp and clatter of the dancers' clogs followed him.

High above, in the shell of the old castle, the Wiccans of Hastings were gathering, their faces grim. The craft stalls were set up now: books and pottery, T-shirts and cards laid out on trestle tables, striped awnings flapping in the breeze off the sea. The followers of the Craft moved among the tourists, nodding to each other, touching an arm here, exchanging a word of encouragement there. The sloping banks of grass around the amphitheater were dotted with spectators now, and a growing crowd surrounded the stage in the center. Morris dancers rubbed shoulders with bikers, New Age pagans with tourists pointing camcorders at the strange sights. A girl dressed as a fairy, shocking pink hair to match her tutu and fishnets, chatted with a man dressed entirely in silver, his skin painted to match. A man in medieval costume and a cloak of green cloth leaves wore the head and pelt of a stag as a headdress, skin and antlers intact, glassy eyes staring. The atmosphere was festive, as befitted a holiday, tinged with the anticipation of the coming of the May King.

Over by Megan's stall, Mrs. P. looked around at the

happy, harmless, eccentric brew of humanity swirling in the cauldron of the castle and smiled.

"Are you OK?" asked Megan.

"Sorry? Oh, yes, dear," replied Mrs. P. dabbing at her eyes. "Just nerves. I'll be fine."

Megan flashed her an uncertain smile and returned to her own worries. On the far side of the castle grounds, Mr. Macmillan watched them with dark intensity.

❖

Charly and Sam stayed close together, fearing that at any moment the Lady Una would return. The flickering light of the sparse torches made shadows leap and dance in every corner, sending their hearts racing as they moved deeper into the earth.

Suddenly, Sam stopped dead and held a hand out behind him, motioning for Charly to do the same. Then she heard it—footsteps, a single set as far as she could tell. Sam raised the athame before him, trying to hold it with authority. The steps grew nearer, fast and purposeful. An elongated shadow played on the wall in front of them. Then, around the corner, a figure came into view, silhouetted against the light of a torch.

"Ah, there you are," said a familiar voice. "You're going the wrong way. Come along!"

"Amergin!" shouted Sam and Charly simultaneously. Charly ran forward and hugged the bard, almost lifting him off his feet.

Disentangling himself with difficulty, Amergin said, "There's no time for all that. We must return to Hastings.

I have been very, very foolish."

"Did you hear that?" asked Charly. "Foolish. He said so himself. Make a note."

"Yup," replied Sam, "heard it with my own ears. It's official."

"Oh, come along, you two," said Amergin, smiling despite himself. "The Sidhe are heading for the castle to sabotage the festival. We have wasted too much time already."

As the wizard led them through the labyrinth of tunnels, they chattered excitedly, recounting their adventures. Amergin muttered with concern as they described the opening of the Gate of Air.

"This crop circle you describe," he mused, "this phenomenon concerns me. Finnvarr said that the Old Ways—the ley lines, you would call them—are full to overflowing with energy since the power of the Malifex was dispersed. I fear these crop circles are a manifestation of that. The land is saturated with power. Any attempt to use the Craft may attract that surplus power like a lightning strike. You had a fortunate escape, my friend."

Charly drew gasps and a "Wow!" from Sam as she described her initiation and her encounter with the Goddess Epona. She secretly hoped that he was slightly jealous, but to her disappointment, he just seemed impressed.

When Sam described his escape from the Sidhe into the ancient forest of the Weald, Charly asked, "If you can make a door anywhere you want, to any place or time, just by thinking about it, why can't you make a door to Hastings, just here for instance?" She gestured at a nearby wall.

"We are still deep within the realm of the Sidhe," explained Amergin. "These are internal walls. A doorway here would simply lead us to the next room."

"Yeah, that's right," agreed Sam, as if the answer had been on the tip of his tongue. Charly sighed. They paced onward in silence.

᛭

Charly began to recognize her surroundings. They were passing through the heartland of the Faery Folk, close by the feasting hall. Beyond that, she was in unfamiliar territory, relying on Amergin's instincts. The wizard seemed far more purposeful than she had seen him for a long time, more like the Amergin who had led her and Sam in their quest against the Malifex. From time to time, however, he would mutter under his breath, "Foolish, foolish."

Puzzled, Charly said, "We've told you most of what happened to us. What about you? What have you done that was so foolish?"

Amergin sighed. "Lost sight of my appointed task, child. Let that be a lesson to you, Sam," he called over his shoulder. "I allowed myself to be distracted by the flash and glitter of your modern world. I forgot my mission to train a hero for the battle against evil. Never again. Buffy!" he exclaimed. "Ha!"

Charly looked at Sam, who shrugged.

Moving on, they entered an area given over to the practice of war—barracks with row after row of low, hard beds; huge, empty stables; vast armories with all but a handful of weapons missing from their racks. Finally, they came to a low doorway, a rectangle of deeper darkness in the general gloom. Amergin held up a hand for them to slow down and approached the doorway cautiously. After a moment, he beckoned them forward, whispering, "We must be silent. There is something evil within, but our way lies beyond this door."

With a feeling of mounting dread, Charly and Sam followed the bard through the doorway. The darkness within was unrelieved by torches, but after a moment, their eyes began to adjust. They were in a cavern, long and broad, with stalactites dripping from the half-glimpsed roof high above. And they were not alone.

It seemed that the Sidhe had taken only their horses to war, leaving their other pets behind. In the half-light, Charly recognized the creatures that had pursued her to the feasting hall of Lord Finnvarr and then mysteriously vanished. The ebb and flow of their breath filled the chamber as, in the gloom, they slept.

Amergin raised a finger to his lips, though neither Sam nor Charly had any intention of making a noise. They were both frozen with dread, staring wide-eyed at the seemingly endless ranks of horrors.

Nearest to the central path sprawled untidy heaps of unclean bodies. Goblins and boggarts were asleep in a tangle of limbs. Scattered among them were the midnight black forms of the cu sith, their huge canine heads on their paws and tongues lolling in the dirt. Farther back in the gloom were larger shapes: the mounded backs of great black bulls and rams—the bugganes—lost in evil dreams. And finally, in the shadowy recesses of the cavern, sights that made Sam bite off a cry of horror: huge and formless in the darkness, the towering figures of giants and trolls, their snores rumbling through the very foundations of the cave.

Charly and Sam exchanged glances, each seeking reassurance in the other's eyes. Then they turned to follow Amergin as he stepped softly along the central path.

In places, the tangle of goblin bodies spilled out in front of them, and they were forced to pick their way through a maze of hairy arms and dark, misshapen legs. Charly's heart threatened to leap out of her chest whenever a goblin stirred and grunted in its sleep. At one point, Sam came perilously close to treading on clawlike fingers as a boggart flopped its arm out in front of him. But the creatures of the Sidhe were deep in slumber, and gradually, the three made progress toward the far end of the chamber.

Suddenly Amergin waved a hand behind him, gesturing for Sam and Charly to stop. Peering around his back, they saw the problem. Blocking the path was a shaggy black mound—one of the cu sith, a dog the size of a horse, built like an Irish wolfhound but with the muscular bulk of a rottweiler. It lay on its side across the path, and it was hunting in its dreams, whimpering softly, its paws and eyebrows twitching as it pursued some unfortunate prey through the forests of its mind.

Amergin gestured toward the belly of the dog, miming that they should try to step between its legs and over its tail. When Sam and Charly nodded that they understood, he set off, slowly and smoothly, testing each footstep before he committed his weight, eyes glued to the dog's legs for signs of movement. And then he was past, and it was

Charly's turn. She placed one foot in the space between the hound's chin and chest, made sure of her balance, and prepared to step over the forelegs. She had one foot in the air when the dog's nostrils began to twitch, and it let out a long, high whimper. Charly froze, teetering on one leg. Gradually, the whimper trailed away, and the dog settled back into sleep. Charly put her foot down next to the huge chest with relief. With more confidence, she stepped along the length of the dog's belly, over its hind legs and tail, and was greeted with a silent hug from Amergin.

Sam had been watching Charly's progress carefully and realized that the first step had to be swift, otherwise his scent would linger before the sleeping hound's nose for too long. Moving boldly, he strode past the head and over the forelegs. The dog remained silent. Pausing beside the slowly heaving chest, Sam scrubbed at his nose with the back of his hand and contemplated the next step. One huge hind leg was pawing at the ground as the dog chased its dream prey. Sam moved closer, waiting for the motion to subside. He sniffed—the noise loud in the silence—and received a glare from Amergin. The leg ceased its frantic twitching, and Sam stepped over, skipped lightly over the tail, and joined the others. And then he sneezed, a huge, unexpected sneeze that bounced off the walls of the cavern and receded into the distance.

"Sam! You idiot!" hissed Charly.

"I can't help it!" he whispered in reply. "I'm allergic to dogs!"

"Well, why didn't you—?"

But Charly was cut off by a high, drawn-out wail. Up

near the roof of the cavern, where stalactites hung in great, fluted curtains, something was stirring. One by one, more of the unearthly cries sprang up around the cavern as the banshees awoke. Upside down, their long, black hair falling around their beautiful faces, they crawled down the stalactites and launched themselves into the air. As they swooped and wheeled around the chamber, wailing and screeching, the other creatures of the Sidhe began to stir.

chapter 8

The procession wound through the streets of Hastings, its numbers swollen now by curious holidaymakers. Despite the overcast sky and a chill wind from the sea, the town was filled with holiday bustle, and the revelers made slow progress through the crowds.

Along the seafront and into the Old Town they made their way, the towering figure of Jack-in-the-Green, like an animated Christmas tree topped with a crown and ribbons, at the head. Behind him came his bogies, clad in vibrant green, adorned with sprigs of vegetation, antlers, and horns. With them came the chimney sweeps, black-clad and sooty-faced, and a red-faced man with a drum, who wore a parody of a military uniform. Drums, large and small, appeared throughout the procession, all of them pounding out the same primeval rhythm. There were giants too, towering figures of papier-mâché; a knight with red hair and beard, brandishing a sword and shield; a witch in a black dress, with ruby lips and huge, dark eyes; a hooded man, all in green. The giants swayed and lurched above the heads of the crowd, while the hobby horse danced around them, sinister in its long black cape. It chased after children who screamed at its snapping jaw and sad, mad eyes.

From time to time, at prearranged points, the procession would stop to rest. Then the music of accordions and pipes began, and morris dancers in crisp white costumes would wheel and spin, bells jingling and ribbons streaming behind them. Above the music and dancing towered Jack, silent and enigmatic beneath his leaves. And whenever the procession moved on, more tourists followed, infected by the feeling that something was imminent, that they were part of some drama that would play out its final act when Jack-in-the-Green reached his destination.

╂╂

High above the streets of town, beneath a gray lid of clouds, the green bowl of the castle was beginning to fill up as tourists and revelers poured in through the gate. The deck chairs around the central stage were all occupied, and the slopes beneath the high circling walls were thick with picnickers. Megan was doing a brisk trade, trying to smile at the customers, but half of her attention was on the crowd. Here and there, she could make out familiar faces, practitioners of the Craft who dropped in and out of the Aphrodite Guest House as if it were their second home. They all had heeded Mrs. P.'s call, and all had the same look, a tightness around the eyes and mouth, their auras filled with expectation, tension, fear. But it was Mrs. P. who caused Megan the greatest concern. Her aura showed all of those things and something more. Something dark and cold—a great, bottomless sadness.

Megan shuddered as she handed a customer his change.

╉╋╉

"What now?" demanded Charly, looking from Sam to Amergin.

The bard peered into the darkness, where huge figures were lurching out of the shadows. "I think," he began carefully, "that we should run."

"And that's the wizard's approach, is it?" Charly snapped.

"There is a time for magic," replied Amergin, breaking into a jog, "and a time for running. And now is definitely running time. MOVE!"

Charly started to follow Amergin, then realized that Sam had remained behind. Turning, she saw that he was rooted to the spot, and she understood why. The floor of the cavern behind them seemed to writhe as hundreds of goblins and boggarts shook off sleep and began to scramble to their feet. High above, one of the banshees wheeled and began to plummet toward them, a terrible scream trailing out behind it. Sam's eyes grew wider as it arrowed toward him, long black hair snapping in the wind of its flight. In a face of porcelain skin and perfect features, blood red lips were pulled back to reveal sharp fangs.

"Come on!" shouted Charly, grabbing Sam by the arm. He stumbled backward, and the banshee hissed past his face, its talons millimeters from his eyes. Gagging on the stench from its black robes, he turned and broke into a run behind Charly, who was sprinting down the chamber toward the retreating figure of Amergin.

The cavern began to echo with cries as the cu sith awoke and began to bay, and the boggarts called to each other in harsh voices. The bugganes lumbered from their resting places, shifting shape from bull to ram to foul goblin form, and in the farthest shadows, the first of the trolls lurched into motion.

✦

The procession left the busy shopping streets along the seafront and turned inland. To the hypnotic pounding of the drums, the holidaymakers and morris dancers, bogies, and giants began their final ascent. The stragglers were still setting off from the seafront as the leaders of the throng began to make their way up Castle Hill, so long had the procession become. High above, a thrill of excitement ran through the crowd assembled in the castle grounds as the word spread: Jack was on his way.

✦

From deep within the Hollow Hills, the Host of the Sidhe rode forth. Lord Finnvarr and Lady Una were at its head, mounted on black steeds with eyes of flame. Behind them rode fifty of the Faery Folk, and twice as many again were on foot—almost all that remained of that race—dressed for war. The hoofs of their horses struck sparks from the stone floor as they made their way toward the human world.

✦

Sam and Charly scrambled over boulders and dodged

around stalagmites as they struggled to catch up with Amergin. The moisture that had created the spires of rock by its slow, millennial dripping made every surface slippery, and both Sam and Charly had lost their footing. Charly had cracked her shin painfully on a rock ledge. But the hoarse breath and howling of the cu sith was close behind them, spurring them on. As they reached the farther end of the cavern, the walls drew closer and the floor became more broken. Amergin was slowing down as the terrain became rougher, and soon Charly and Sam caught up with him.

Turning to them, he cried, "Duck!" and they felt a gust of foul air as two of the banshees swooped over them. Amergin let loose a bolt of energy from his fingertips, dropping one of the creatures with a shriek. They heard a sickening crack as it collided with a spire of rock.

"Come on!" shouted Amergin. "I can see a way out." He pointed ahead to a narrow crack of deeper darkness toward the cavern's end. Sam and Charly scrambled after him as he picked his way through the tumbled rock debris toward the opening. Sam heard a clatter of stone and turned. The cu sith were close now, claws skittering on the damp rock, their tongues lolling from their mouths and their jaws flecked with foam. And behind them came the goblins and boggarts, a foul tide sweeping over every surface, some running upright, some scuttling on all fours, trampling each other in their haste to reach their quarry. The air resounded with harsh cries in nameless languages, the furious baying of the cu sith, and farther off but drawing nearer, the rumbling bellows of trolls.

The nearest of the great black dogs scented victory and made a huge bound forward, its eyes blazing red in the darkness. It landed close behind Sam, who was struggling to move at speed over the wet rubble of the cavern floor. Amergin had reached the opening in the cave wall and paused. Turning, he saw the massive hound bearing down on Sam. Pulling Charly to him, he flung out one hand and sent forth a blast of violet energy, but at that moment, the dog slipped and crashed to the floor. The bolt of energy passed over its head, and then it was on its feet once more, talons scrabbling as it fought for a footing. As Sam sprinted the last few agonizing meters to the exit, the claws of the cu sith caught on solid rock and it sprang forward, jaws agape. Charly reached for Sam's hand and dragged him into the opening in the cavern wall. The faery hound, unable to stop its momentum, crashed headlong into the opening and slumped to the ground, its massive head and shoulders blocking half the exit.

"That should hold off some of the others," shouted Amergin, and he set off along a narrow passageway. Charly cast a concerned eye over the white-faced Sam, then turned to follow the bard.

✝✝

The procession picked its way up the entrance track to the castle and paused at the ticket office. The papier-mâché giants—the knight, the black-clad Morrigan, old Hannah Clarke the witch—were manhandled to the ground and reverently passed through the entrance. Once inside, they were hefted aloft once more and the procession moved on. A thrill passed through the crowd as the first drummers and morris dancers appeared inside the castle wall. Jack was coming.

┽┾

On the summit of West Hill, under the blank-eyed gaze of the guesthouses, was a wide, grassy, open space known as the Ladies Parlor. Once it had hosted tournaments for the nearby castle and resounded to the clash of jousting knights. Now it was the preserve of dog walkers and kite flyers. The wind, wet from the sea, hissed through the short grass, bowling stray candy wrappers across the expanse of green. Scattered leaves and pieces of paper swirled, dancing together in the air. A pattern began to emerge, a stately rotation of debris, scraps of litter tracing the edges of a wide vortex.

The pace of the wind increased, lashing the grass in a broad circle, dust and twigs spiraling faster around a point in the center of the Ladies Parlor. And then they came.

From the heart of the whirlwind rode the Host of the Sidhe, clad in the full panoply of war. The hoofs of their horses sounded like thunder on the hard turf, and the thin gray light glinted on jeweled bridles as Finnvarr, King of the Host of the Air, led his people to war. By his side, the Lady Una shook her long black hair free in the sea wind and laughed, high and cruel. In response, her steed tossed its head and snorted, fire jetting from its nostrils. The shouts of tourists in the distance, converging on the castle for the festival, mingled with the crying of the gulls.

Finnvarr reined in his horse and paused for a moment,

looking back at the assembled throng, the last of their race. Then turning his gaze to the castle entrance, he cried out in the ancient tongue of the Tuatha de Danaan—a battle cry from the old days, before the coming of the Milesians—and the Host rode on.

✛

Sam and Charly followed Amergin through a complex maze of tunnels. They were leaving behind the realm of the Sidhe. The passageways here had been little modified, merely cleared of the worst obstacles. Often they were forced to crawl on hands and knees or squeeze themselves through cracks in the dripping rock. When they paused to tackle a particularly tricky scramble over fallen boulders, Charly said, "On my way in here, I turned into a bat."

"What do you mean, *turned into?*" Sam asked with a smirk on his face. Charly ignored him.

"I turned into a bat," she continued, "and it was much easier. You can get through tiny gaps, and you can see everything. Well, sort of see . . . or hear . . ." She trailed off.

"Hm-m-m," pondered Amergin. "It's not a bad idea, but I fear it would not serve us now. To find an exit from the Hollow Hills, we will need our human senses. No, I fear we must stay as we were born, though it grieves me to move so slowly." He paused, holding up a hand.

Charly and Sam heard the approaching sound of voices, harsh and cruel. The goblins, being smaller than humans and accustomed to their subterranean home, could move more rapidly. They had passed the obstacle of the fallen cu sith and were drawing near.

"Come," continued Amergin. He stooped, cupping his hands together, the fingers interlaced. Charly placed one foot into Amergin's firm grip and felt herself hoisted upward. Scrambling onto the top of a slab of fallen rock, she gazed back into the threatening darkness as Sam and Amergin joined her. Then they were off once more, slipping and stumbling on weary legs through the broken landscape.

✛

Most of the procession had dispersed into the castle grounds, to the craft stalls and refreshment tent, leaving Jack and his followers to pick their way up the slope of grass at the rear of the amphitheater. Here they paused, resting high above the revelers, while morris dancers took their turn upon the stage below.

Down on her stall, Megan could bear it no longer. Ignoring the waiting customers, she fled into the crowd. To one side of the castle, behind a stall selling cards and T-shirts, was an area where the giants had been abandoned. They looked strangely forlorn, propped against the pitted stonework, their time of glory over. It was here that she found Mrs. P.

The old lady was gazing at the pale paper features of the Morrigan, black hair and black dress contrasting sharply with her white skin. Without looking around, she said, "I used to look like her once, my sweet. You may find that hard to believe now." She turned to smile at Megan. Tears glistened on her cheeks. "They're close now," she continued. "I can feel them."

Megan reached out and touched Mrs. P.'s arm, and suddenly they were hugging, the old woman's head buried against Megan's chest. When she finally looked up, Megan barely recognized her. Mrs. P. seemed to have aged a decade in a matter of seconds.

Mrs. P. sighed. "I'm sorry, my dear. I'm just a foolish old woman. Age is supposed to bring wisdom, but some days I think it only brings rheumatism and a tendency to forget where you left things."

"It's going to be fine," said Megan, squeezing Mrs. P.'s shoulders.

"Of course it is, lovey. Of course it is. Come on. We must get ready."

Megan gave her what she hoped was a reassuring smile, turned, and headed back into the crowd.

Mrs. P. watched her for a moment, then muttered under her breath, "Lady, grant me the strength to leave them behind." And then she set off, a tiny figure beneath the towering giants.

-+-+-

The Host of the Sidhe crossed the road, their horses oblivious to the screeching of car brakes and the screams of fleeing tourists. Faces stern and pale, they made their way along the narrow track that led to the castle entrance. Up ahead, at the entrance to the castle, King Finnvarr saw an obstacle: the low, wooden ticket office that spanned the narrow gap in the stone walls. He reined in his horse and stared for a moment. Then he raised one hand in the air, palm upward and fingers clawed. The wind began to gust, swirling savagely in the confined space. Gradually, the ragged gusts gathered into a whirlwind, a screaming funnel of air that tracked slowly across the ground, clouds of dust billowing at its feet. With a horrifying inevitability, it smashed into the ticket office. There was a rending sound, a shattering of glass, and a chorus of screams. Chunks of timber flew out into the track, one clattering to a halt at the feet of Finnvarr's horse.

Finnvarr lowered his hand and the twister dispersed. Paper leaflets advertising local attractions fluttered to the ground like autumn leaves. Finnvarr tapped his heels against his mount's flanks, and the Host of the Sidhe moved on.

✛

The goblins were close now, the scrambling sound of their feet and hands like a rising tide in the narrow tunnel. Charly, Amergin, and Sam were battered and weary, the palms of their hands scraped raw by the rock, their shins bruised and aching.

"We're nearly there," gasped Amergin. "I can feel the outer world drawing close. Sam, you must use your power."

Sam stared at his feet, panting helplessly.

"Sam? Come on! We need your power." Charly shook him by the shoulder. His head wobbled up, and he looked at her blankly.

"Power?"

"You are a Walker Between Worlds, my friend," said Amergin kindly. "Come—find us a doorway."

Behind them, goblins and bugganes began to spill through a narrow gap between two stalagmites. A crude bronze knife struck the rock by Charly's face, showering her with dust. She helped Amergin to push Sam into the lead. He stumbled forward, hands groping blindly along the walls of the passage. And then he collided with something: a blank wall of stone.

"It's a dead end," he mumbled and then louder, "It's a dead end!"

"Come on, Sam," hissed Charly. "You're the hero—do something!"

"I'm not." He sighed, "I . . . I don't know how."

The nearest goblins saw that they had halted and soon realized why. Knowing that they had their prey cornered, they slowed. Despite their vast numbers, they were wary, edging forward, tittering and hissing with anticipation.

"Charly," said Amergin, "we must help him. Take his shoulder." He placed one hand on Sam's shoulder, gesturing for Charly to do the same. Leaning close to Sam, he said quietly, "Sam, my friend, only you can do this, but we can help. Take our strength. Find us a way."

"Quickly!" shouted Charly. A boggart, bigger and bolder than the rest, was shuffling toward them with a sideways gait, ready to turn and run, but with a glint of bloodlust in its eyes. It made lunging motions with a dagger as it came, hissing through yellow teeth.

Sam shut his eyes, sending his thoughts out into the rock. He tried to recall what it had felt like when he had found his way into the ancient Weald, spilling out onto the sunny grass of the South Downs with the mighty forest stretched out before him. But all he could remember was a feeling of fear, of overwhelming need. The stone beneath his hand felt like stone, nothing more—just the old familiar crystal tang of ancient bedrock.

Suddenly, Charly screamed. The boggart had reached her and grabbed her by the arm. Frantically, she tried to beat it off while still clinging with one hand to Sam's shoulder. "Sam," she sobbed. "Now!"

For a split second, Sam turned and saw the leering face of the boggart bearing down on Charly, the bronze dagger raised to strike. He closed his eyes, turned back to the rock, and pushed.

He stumbled, lost his footing, and fell, rolling forward. He felt the comforting hands on his shoulders wrenched free, but then something solid rose up and struck him on the temple, and he sank into oblivion.

+++

Up on the high slope within the castle yard, Jack's followers began to drum. With looks of intense purpose, they fell into a particular rhythm, throbbing and somehow primeval. Drummers all around the castle heard the rhythm and synchronized with it, until the whole green bowl of the ancient site seemed to pulsate to the sound. It could be felt in the chest, in the time-worn stone walls, in the old bones of the West Hill itself.

Then Jack began to move. Slowly, with great dignity, the towering green figure made its way down the winding path in the castle grounds to the central stage, and there he took up his position. Surrounded by his followers, he dominated the crowd, ancient and enigmatic, a faceless green cone of vegetation, ribbons fluttering in the breeze. The pounding of the drums rose to a crescendo and abruptly ceased. Silence fell. A single female voice, high and pure, was raised in song, bidding farewell to the winter, yearning for the summer that would soon be set free by the ritual destruction of Jack-in-the-Green.

But something was wrong. Screams could be heard from outside the castle walls and a crashing sound, the shattering of glass. The crowd around the stage began to exchange worried looks. Some of the tourists smiled, thinking that this was part of the day's entertainment, some sort of historical reenactment.

The screaming outside grew more intense, and a cloud of dust could be seen at the entrance. Then the ticket office exploded, sending fragments of wood into the air. The crowd panicked, but there was nowhere to run. The only way in or out was through the ticket office. A few people set off in that direction anyway, despite the screams coming from its shattered remains. But they soon halted in their tracks. For out of the dust came figures from a dream—the Faery Folk, riding abroad in the mortal world, fire flickering around the mouths of their horses.

Silence fell, broken by sobs. Side by side, King Finnvarr and the Lady Una rode into the castle grounds.

✢

Charly opened her eyes. "It hasn't worked!" she cried in dismay. They were clearly still in the caves. She was at the foot of a wall of rock, in some kind of narrow crevice.

There was one improvement, though—light was shining down on her. Her eyes tracked upward, and she screamed. Above her head, jammed into a narrow chimney of rock, was a skeleton. It was suspended, face down, in some sort of iron cage, tattered scraps of clothing and pale bones hanging above her. She jumped to her feet and scuttled backward, tripping over Sam's inert body. He groaned, shaking his head. Putting a hand to his temple, he felt something wet and a dull ache.

"We're still in the caves!" shouted Charly, to nobody in particular. "It hasn't worked, and now we're going to be too late!"

Sam peered back into the recess from which Charly had emerged and found Amergin sitting up, rubbing his head.

"Come on," said Sam, "Charly says we're still in the caves. We'd better get going before those . . . *things* catch up."

He pulled Amergin to his feet, and together they set off after Charly. Crossing the floor of a broad, smooth-floored chamber, they heard an urgent hiss and ran toward its source. They found Charly by the door of a side chamber. She waved for them to slow down and to stay quiet, then gestured into the open doorway. Sam tiptoed forward and peered around the edge of the opening. He jerked his head back, eyes wide with surprise. There were people in the small room, definitely human, bent over something as if deep in concentration. Charly followed him. She frowned for a moment, then chuckled.

"It's OK," she said loudly, "come and see." And she strode into the room. When Sam and Amergin caught up with her, she was kicking one of the figures in the seat of its pants.

"What are they?" asked Sam. "Pirates?"

"Smugglers," replied Charly, leaning on one of the wax dummies, a man in a baggy white shirt and leather waistcoat.

"Smugglers? But . . . Oh, the Smugglers Caves."

"Can somebody tell me what's going on?" asked Amergin forlornly.

"We're in the Smugglers Caves," explained Charly. "It's a tourist attraction, exhibits of what the place looked like when these caves were used by smugglers to store their contraband. It's just by the—"

"The castle entrance!" exclaimed Sam. "We're right by the castle! Come on!"

Minutes later, the ticket attendant of the Smugglers Caves looked up from her newspaper as three ragged, dusty figures, one with blood on his face, hurtled up the long passageway and out through the exit. As the turnstile clicked to a halt, she sat in bewilderment. She was sure that the last few visitors had left about fifteen minutes earlier.

✛✛✛

As the Host of the Sidhe rode into the castle grounds, Megan, Mrs. P., and their fellow Wiccans had moved into position. Pushing through the frightened crowd, they formed a circle around the center stage, backs to the towering figure of Jack-in-the-Green. To their credit, his bogies had stayed by his side, clustered together on the stage, shooting fearful glances around the amphitheater. Mrs. P. went to them and spoke with their leader, who

169

nodded several times, his mouth set in a grim line. Then she returned to the circle of Wiccans. Megan, meanwhile, had gone in search of the girl who had sung the song that welcomed the coming summer. She found her, pale-faced and shaking, over by a blue-and-white striped pavilion. After a few seconds of intense discussion, Megan led her by the hand back to the stage.

✛•✛

Sam, Charly, and Amergin ran up the sloping track that led from the Smugglers Caves and clattered up a flight of steps onto the windy summit of West Hill. In front of them was the green expanse of the Ladies Parlor. To their left, unseen, was the entrance to the castle. Screams carried to them on the breeze.

"Come," said Amergin. "We may yet be in time." With that, he disappeared, and in his place was a bird of prey, steely blue gray above, palest buff below, flecked with dark markings. With a swirling feeling of dislocation, Sam and Charly found themselves transformed, and together the three merlins took to the sky.

✛•✛

The frightened crowd pulled back as Lord Finnvarr walked his horse forward toward the stage. Behind him came the Lady Una and the rest of the Host, the hoofs of their mounts clicking softly on the ancient stones.

By the stage, Megan whispered, "Now—sing!" and the young woman began her song once more, her voice quavering at first but growing in strength. Into the silence she poured the words, a challenge to the forces of winter, a hymn of praise to the coming May King.

Finnvarr smiled.

✛✛✛

High above the castle, Amergin paused in his flight, hovering for a moment on the wind from the sea. One obsidian eye took in the scene below. With a fierce cry, he folded back his wings and plunged, arrowing down toward the circle of stones below. Close behind him came Sam and Charly.

✛✛✛

The song ended, and the time had come to release the summer. "Now!" shouted Mrs. P., gesturing to her fellow Wiccans. They moved toward the figure of Jack, to take apart his body, leaf and branch, and distribute them to the crowd.

Finnvarr swung one leg over his horse's broad back and dropped to the ground. The slap of his boots on the hard earth rang out in the silence. Striding toward the stage, he called out, "No, old woman! Not this time. This time, the job falls to me." And he drew a long, bronze sword from a black leather scabbard at his hip.

Behind him, twenty or so of his followers dismounted and drew their blades. Those who remained on horseback moved off into the crowd, spreading out around the central stage, forming a circle with Jack at its heart. The crowd scrambled to get out of their way, screaming as the fiery breath of the horses moved among them. The

171

Wiccans on the stage froze with indecision, looking from Mrs. P. to the approaching faeries.

A shriek rang out, high above. Three sleek shapes plummeted toward the earth, wings arched back, talons outstretched. At the last moment, when it seemed they must surely hit the ground, there was a shimmer of air, and there stood Amergin, Sam, and Charly.

"Finnvarr of the Sidhe," called out Amergin, "That power is not yours to take. Leave it be."

Finnvarr threw back his head and laughed. "You? Once more you come to meddle in the fate of my people?" He turned to Amergin. "Have you not caused us enough hurt?"

Amergin shrugged. "What is done is done. But for this moment, I will do what I must to stop you."

"You are alone now, old bard," sneered the Lord of the Sidhe. "The heroes of Mil are long turned to dust, and your time is past. Leave the future to such as these." He gestured around. "Frightened cattle, with their trinkets and superstitions. They deserve to be led."

"Not by such as you," replied Amergin quietly. "Like me, your time is past. Go back to your hills."

"Oh, no." Finnvarr shook his head. "We will hide no more!" And with that, he thrust forward his left hand. A gust of wind, tightly focused, hit Amergin square in the chest, sending him sprawling.

Over by the stage, Megan cried out, "Amergin!" and began to push her way through the crowd toward him.

The Faeries who were on foot began to move, some rallying to the side of their lord, some moving toward the stage. Sam decided to take advantage of the confusion and made his way through the crowd, heading for the silent figure of Jack-in-the Green.

Charly, hearing her mother's cry, set off toward her but found her way blocked. "You," she sighed.

"Not pleased to see me, girly?" asked the Lady Una with a smirk. She hit Charly with a blast of air that sent her skidding across the ground. Charly scrambled to her feet, desperately trying to think of a way to defend herself. But she was still very new to her powers. Shape-shifting was an effort, and she had no experience at all of protective magic, never mind spells of attack. She put out a hand before her, trying to picture in her mind the sort of defensive shield she had seen Amergin use. But no sooner had the image formed than she was knocked backward once more. The Lady Una smiled to herself.

Sam pushed his way through the crush, trying to keep Jack in view. But the Sidhe had spotted him. From all sides, tall Faeries were heading in his direction, kicking and elbowing frightened onlookers from their path. Sam glanced back. One Faery was very close, a leaf-shaped bronze dagger drawn in readiness to strike. Turning once more to the stage, Sam gasped as a bulky figure stepped in front of him. "You!" he gasped. "I knew it!"

It was Mr. Macmillan, the sinister guest from the Aphrodite Guest House. Beneath his greasy black hair and bushy eyebrows, his face was lit up with fierce glee. But to Sam's confusion, he was wearing the costume of a morris dancer, crisp white linen and silver bells, ribbons at his knees and elbows.

"What—?" began Sam.

"Duck!" shouted Mr. Macmillan and lunged over Sam's shoulder.

Sam felt a gust of wind against his neck and turned, but there was nothing there. Looking back, he found Mr. Macmillan wiping a steel kitchen knife on the leg of his trousers.

Still grinning, Mr. Macmillan said, "It works, then— the iron trick. Now, get going, lad! Save Jack. Save the summer!"

Sam stumbled past, mumbling, "Thanks! Sorry..." Rather too late, he remembered Wayland's athame, tucked in his belt, and drew it.

All around the stage, the Wiccans of southern England were defending Jack. With kitchen knives and iron pokers, with bunches of herbs and wands of rowan wood they beat back the Sidhe. Mrs. P. ran to and fro, shouting out orders, sending her friends and colleagues to block gaps in their defenses, distributing bunches of herbs: vervain and Saint-John's-wort. Whenever one of the Faery Folk fell to the bite of iron, his passing was marked by a gust of wind and a high, thin scream. But weight of numbers was on their side, and slowly they closed in toward the figure of Jack.

Amergin and Finnvarr were locked in a battle of their own. Oblivious to the activity by the stage, they thrust and parried, bolts of crackling energy and blasts of air detonating around them. Then something came into the corner of Finnvarr's vision, and he paused. Whirling around, he seized Megan and pressed the blade of his sword to her throat. "This one means something to you, I think," he growled to Amergin. "Let this be a lesson to you, bard.

Never become too attached to mortals. They are so very . . . breakable." And with that he began to edge toward the stage, the blade against Megan's neck and one of her arms wrenched painfully up her back. Amergin looked on in despair.

Charly too was taking a beating. She had hit her head against an ancient cobblestone and was having trouble focusing her eyes. And while she struggled to rally her senses, Una laid into her again and again. One particularly well-aimed gust of air hit her in the stomach and dropped her to the ground, gasping for breath. She fell back, panting, staring upward. The Lady Una came into view, standing above her with the familiar smirk on her face. Something crystallized within Charly. It was the old, instinctive hatred for Una, the cold loathing that had gripped Charly as she stood in the line for the East Hill Cliff Railway. Keeping her face carefully neutral, she thought, *Right, lady—there's more than one way to tackle this*. If magic didn't work, there were older, simpler ways.

Charly groaned and rolled her head from side to side, but she continued to watch Una through slitted eyes. As the Faery Queen leaned closer, Charly brought her knees up to her chest and kicked out with all her strength, catching Una in the pit of the stomach. The breath hissed out of her, and she staggered backward, sitting down with a heavy thud. Charly sprang to her feet and brushed herself down, muttering, "See how you like it!" Then, as Una fought to regain her breath, Charly closed her eyes and centered herself. Casting her mind back to that night on the Firehills, she tried to recall how it had felt when she had carried out the ritual of Drawing Down the Moon. There was no time to go through the words of the ceremony now. She would have to try to capture the essence. She struggled. So much had happened since then. Una was on her feet again, a look of white-hot fury on her face. And then it came to Charly—the smell of coconut, the fragrance of a million gorse flowers pouring their scent into the night sky.

As if the memory of that smell had unlocked a door, the sensation of heightened awareness came over her again, every nerve in her body attuned to its surroundings. She could see, hear, smell, feel everything so intensely it was almost painful. And with this sensation came a slowing down of time. Una was drawing back one hand, preparing to strike at Charly with the power of the gale. But she moved as if in slow motion. Charly had plenty of time to turn toward the central stage, where Sam had spotted her. He cried out, a long, low drone of sound, and raised a languid arm. Something left his hand and drifted through the air toward her. She reached up and plucked the athame from its lazy arc, then turned to Una. From the palm of the Faery's upturned hand, a vortex of air was spreading, shimmering ripples spiraling out toward her. Casually, Charly threw up a shield, a shimmering web of green force that deflected the blast of air with ease. With an effort of will, she returned time to its normal speed. Calmly, she faced her enemy. She was Charly, but she was also Epona, horse goddess of the Celts, and she was armed with iron. It was time to fight back.

Sam looked around. Charly seemed to be doing fine

now that she had his athame, but he was in a rather worse predicament. The Sidhe were converging on him from all sides, despite the best efforts of the Wiccans. Suddenly, there was a tug at his elbow. He looked down into the wrinkled face of Mrs. P.

"Go to Jack, lovey," she pleaded. "Set free the summer."

"But—" began Sam, gesturing at the advancing faeries.

"Don't worry about them. We'll take care of them."

And as Sam scrambled to the edge of the stage, Mrs. P. made her stand against the Host.

Finnvarr had reached the edge of the stage now, the frightened Wiccans backing away from the cold threat of the blade against Megan's neck. With difficulty, he scrambled up, dragging Megan behind him. Close by, Sam too climbed up onto the stage. The Sidhe were almost upon him, and he had given up his one weapon. Still, if he had to give the athame to anybody, he was glad it was Charly. She seemed to be holding her own now against Una, and somehow that gave him strength.

Charly and the Lady Una fought back and forth, oblivious to events at the center of the arena. Charly had mastered her defensive shield now, and she had begun to take the fight to Una, firing bolt after bolt of energy at the Queen of the Sidhe. Also, to distract her opponent, she shifted shape, from deer to boar to hare, flickering through a kaleidoscope of animal forms. Una was weakening, her long black hair in disarray, her clothes dirty and torn. Finally, she felt cold stone against her back. She was cornered, pressed into the junction of two ancient remnants of the castle walls. But then there was a cry, high and despairing. It sounded like the boy, Sam.

Charly turned from her opponent, distracted by the scream, and Una seized her opportunity. A series of rapid blows slammed into Charly, and she fell, tripping over a low stone wall and landing heavily. Una pounced, launching herself at Charly with hands clawed, long red fingernails hooked like talons. At the last moment, Charly brought up the athame. It took Una full in the throat. With her eyes screwed tight, Charly felt a blast of warm air wash over her and heard a long, furious scream that trailed away as if into the far distance. She opened her eyes, and Una was gone. Struggling to her feet, she turned to look at the stage.

Finnvarr flung Megan from him, sending her stumbling over the edge of the low platform, and raced toward Jack. Sam, who had been closer, was there already, standing before the towering cone of foliage and ribbon, one hand outstretched to pluck the first leaf that would free the summer. Finnvarr moaned as he ran, a long, low desperate sound, and lunged with his sword.

Sam's eyes widened with surprise as something cold entered his back, pushing impossibly through and out. There was an unpleasant scrape of metal on bone as the blade was withdrawn but no real pain. Not yet. The pain would come, he was sure. For the moment, though, there was just surprise and a feeling of loss. The world was slipping away, a world that he had once felt so connected to, such a part of. In slow motion, Sam sank to his knees. There seemed to be a wall in front of him, a green wall. He reached out for support, but part of the wall came away in his hand. He hit the boards of the stage, slumping sideways, and just as he slipped out of consciousness, he saw that he was holding a sprig of green.

Finnvarr turned to the horrified crowd, sword raised in triumph. Turning on his heel, he spun, the sword hissing horizontally through the air. Effortlessly, it severed the crowned apex of Jack-in-the-Green from its conical body, narrowly missing the cowering head of the man inside the green framework. With a flutter of leaves and ribbons, the severed crown rolled across the boards and dropped into the crowd.

"Jack is dead!" Finnvarr cried in triumph. "Attis is gone, his power dispersed. The legacy of his dark brother, the Malifex, is ours to claim. Life and death, the cycle of the seasons, they are ours now. Your dominion in this land is over, mortals!"

Sam, in a dark place far away, felt something stir behind him. No, not behind him, for he was turned in upon himself, his senses at an end. Behind his mind, then, something moved—a familiar presence. He thought he heard a chuckle, deep and musical, and perhaps, far off, the sound of pipes and horns. He felt a tingling sensation, reminding him of the flesh that he had so recently left behind. Perhaps it was like the ghostly itches that people felt in limbs that they had lost, old nerves firing from habit. But there it was again, in his fingers, spreading into the palm of his hand. The darkness that had been closing in on Sam receded a little as his curiosity was aroused. There was a definite sensation, spreading up his arm now. *Perhaps I'm not dead after all*, he thought, and with the thought came a further rush of sensation, washing up his arm and into his damaged chest. He opened one eye a crack and peered down the length of his arm, lying limply on the boards of the stage. From fingertips to shoulder, it was covered in green leaves. Sam closed his eyes once more, and in his mind hunting horns were blowing.

Finnvarr pointed to Amergin and shouted, "Bring him here! Bring me the Milesian!" Tall faeries converged on Amergin and seized him by the arms, dragging him toward the stage. Megan tried to pull them off, but they slapped her away as if she were an insect. Amergin was thrown down at Finnvarr's feet.

"Now," began the Lord of the Sidhe, "the time has come for retribution. My first use for the freed power of the Malifex will be to rip the living soul from the last survivor of the race that stole my home and destroyed my people."

"And you're quite sure you have that power?" asked Amergin quietly.

"Of course, fool. The power of the Green Man is ended, the balance destroyed. Nothing stands in my way now."

"I wouldn't be so sure," replied the bard, staring over Finnvarr's shoulder.

Finnvarr turned. Something was rising from the boards of the stage. Indeed, part of it seemed to be made of the boards, the wood blending seamlessly with the leaves that covered its legs. Dense foliage cloaked the arms and torso, but Finnvarr could just make out enough of the face to recognize Sam.

"No!" he cried. "No. It can't be. I killed you."

Leaves spilled out of Sam's mouth and nostrils, and the last traces of his face were hidden. He continued to grow, until he towered over the Lord of the Sidhe.

"No!" repeated Finnvarr. "I will not allow this! I have come too far!" He pulled back one hand, summoning all his power to hurl at the figure of the Green Man. "Rally to me!" he shouted, and the remnants of the Host came running to his side, summoning their own powers to bolster his.

Sam looked down at them, felt the force gathering within them, the ancient might of the wind, strong enough to level forests and wear mountains down to sand. Even he could not face such a blast and survive.

He needed a weapon to replace the athame. He cast about with his mind, sending a tendril of thought down into the soil. He did not have far to look, for the bones of the earth were close to the surface here. He soon tasted rock and sent his thoughts down through it, searching, testing. And there he found it—the familiar blood-tang of iron. He drew the sensation into himself, let it flow through him, until his veins pulsed with a stream of molten metal. He remembered his time with Wayland and the smith's quiet patience as he heated and reheated the iron, tempering it until it was hard but not brittle, flexible yet strong. And when he felt that he had captured that balance within him, that he was tempered like steel, he struck.

The remaining Host of the Sidhe had gathered their power, channeling it through Finnvarr. He stood, eyes ablaze, arms spread wide to summon the whirlwind that would blast the Green Man, Attis, the May King, from the face of the land. His hair streamed out behind him in the gathering storm, and he cried out his triumph.

But before Finnvarr could strike, a wave of force exploded from Sam, the concentrated essence of iron, expanding out through the crowd. Spheres of energy popped into existence around his head, hissing and spitting. A vortex of force began to spin around him. Part of his mind recognized it—the crop circle power. As Amergin had said, the land was overflowing with energy, the dispersed power of the Malifex seeking an outlet. Sam opened himself to it, let it flow through him, mingling it with the taste of the blood-metal. The humans in the crowd flinched as the halo of steel blue light washed over them, and they felt nothing. But as it touched the Host of the Sidhe, they were snuffed out like flames, their forms fraying into smoke, out over the castle walls. For a few moments, their screams rent the air and then faded away, until all that could be heard was the high keening of the gulls.

+++

Sam looked around at the devastation, the frightened faces of the crowd, the exhausted Wiccans gazing up at him. Their expressions frightened him—gratitude and hope, yes, but something else. Then it dawned on him. It was worship. As if he were some kind of god. Panic gripped him. He was only Sam, he didn't want this, had never asked for it. He looked at the sea of faces and tried to think what he could do for them. Then it came to him. There was something that remained unfinished, and it was within his power to finish it. After a moment, he raised one hand, gesturing at the sky, and then sank into the earth without a trace.

Above the castle, the clouds parted, driven inland by a fresh breeze from the sea. The sun broke through, pouring its warmth onto the upturned faces among the ancient rocks.

Summer had come.

╍┼╍

They found Mrs. P. at the foot of the stage, as they were ushering the confused tourists out of the arena. Charly spotted her first and cried out for her mother. But she knew, even before Megan arrived and checked for a pulse. Amergin and Mr. Macmillan helped to carry her body, and a solemn procession of Wiccans accompanied them as they made their way out of the castle and down into the Old Town.

epilogue

They had to tell Sam's parents, in the end, when his father arrived at the Aphrodite Guest House and found he was missing. There followed a period that would always remain a blur in Charly's mind, a time of tears and shouting, confusion and worry. Sam's parents refused to believe the tales of shape-changing and battles against the ancient Sidhe and called the police. But there were too many witnesses to the strange events in the castle, and the authorities soon found themselves out of their depth. The police tried to hush up the whole business, issuing vague statements about mass hysteria and rampaging teenage delinquents. Sam's parents were told to wait—their son would show up when he was good and ready.

+++

Charly, Megan, and Amergin stayed on at the Aphrodite for several weeks, wrapping up Mrs. P.'s affairs, arranging for her funeral. A special ceremony was held, a Wiccan celebration of her life. Megan and Charly cried a great deal, even though they knew Mrs. P. would have been disappointed in them. Charly was welcomed into the

Hastings Wiccan community, taking part in their rites and learning the discipline that, as a new initiate, she had lacked.

But most often she liked to wander on her own, much as she had done back home in Dorset, after her father had left. Megan worried but recognized it as her daughter's way of working things through.

Charly's favorite place was the Firehills.

And it was there, one evening toward the end of her stay, that Sam came to her. He rose out of the ground beside her, wild and wary, his hair a tangle of leaves and a fierce, amber light in his eyes. He shied away as she moved toward him, his shape flickering through a series of half-glimpsed animal forms.

"It's OK," she said softly, standing very still. And then, "I've missed you."

Sam paced back and forth like a caged animal, his eyes darting to Charly's face, then flickering away. Then he stopped, shoulders hunched, eyes closed, and whispered, "Help me."

She went to him and held him close, waiting until the sobs subsided. When she thought that he might be ready to speak, she asked, "Where have you been? We've been worried sick."

"Everywhere," replied Sam. "I've been everywhere. I've traveled the length and breadth of the land, I've been everything—birds, fish, insects . . ." His voice trailed off. "I don't know what to do," he finished in a whisper.

"Sam, what's happened to you? I can't help you if I don't know."

Sam sank to the ground, and Charly sat by his side.

After a while, he began. "It's him—the Green Man again. Do you understand how the festival works?"

Charly shook her head.

"Jack-in-the-Green's just a bloke in a costume, right? Just somebody inside a framework, covered in leaves. So why were the Sidhe so keen to destroy him?"

Charly remained silent, letting Sam work through what he had to say.

"Because, when enough people believe in something, that thing has a power. And for a moment, at the end of the ritual, when everybody is waiting for the summer to be released, that framework of leaves *becomes* something else. It becomes Jack, Attis, the Green Man." He paused. "And I was there, at that moment. I plucked the first leaf, and something happened to me. Probably because of what happened before, because there was a bit of the Green Man inside me already, I don't know. Charly"—he turned to her, amber eyes raw with hurt—"I'm him. The Green Man. I'm him now, completely. Not just a part of him tucked away somewhere at the back of my mind. I'm him, and he's me."

He turned away once more, gazing out over the golden hillside.

"I saw the way they looked at me when the Sidhe had gone. I'm not their god. I'm just a kid. And I don't know what to do."

Charly threw back her head and chuckled. "Poor old Sam," she said with a sigh and clambered to her feet. "What's the matter?" she demanded. "Afraid to be different?"

She called up the spirit of the Goddess, feeling the power of her other mother, Epona the Huntress, flow into her. She grew taller, darker, and the light of a moon that had not yet risen shone from her. "We're all different, kid. Deal with it."

Sam stared at Charly, barely recognizing her. He was torn between wonder and hurt—wonder at what she had become, hurt that she wouldn't take him seriously.

Charly continued. "The thing is, we don't have to deal with it alone."

Sam scowled, but he knew how futile it was to argue with Charly.

"We were never meant to be like everyone else," Charly continued. "You must see that? Everything changed when you woke Amergin and set us on this path. Neither of us can go back to how things were. And it will be hard. Of course, it will. It's always difficult to be different. But we'll get through it, because that's what we do. Don't we?"

Sam stared at the ground, lost in thought. Was it really as simple as Charly said? It was all right for her. She had always been the strong one, through all their adventures. Whereas he was blown along by fate, desperately trying to keep his feet as the tide of events swirled around him. And now he was lost. That was it—lost to himself. His face, when he had glimpsed it in still pools, was familiar, but inside, the landscape of his life had changed. He was neither boy nor man nor god but a little of each. And to survive, he would have to find a balance. He would have help. Amergin and Megan were wise, and Charly—something had happened to Charly too. She would understand what he was going through. He looked up at her then and nodded, smiling despite himself. She held out her hand and hauled him to his feet.

"Now, come on. We've got a lot to talk about," said Charly, and hand in hand, Horse Goddess and Horned God, they walked down through the Firehills toward the sea.

To find out how it all began read

The Malifex
by Steve Alton

Sam just wants to be left alone to play his video games as another boring vacation with his parents looms ahead.

But within days of arriving in southern England, he mistakenly awakes the ancient wizard Amergin from a two-thousand-year sleep. With Amergin, and his new friend Charly, Sam finds himself involved in a timeless battle against the evil Malifex, and his life changes forever.

About the Author

Steve Alton lives in southern England, where he writes in his spare time. He is also a botanical illustrator, a computer graphics artist, and a photographer. He is also the author of *The Malifex,* an earlier book about Sam, Charly, and Amergin.